FORTY-FIVE SUMMERS

Other books by Brian Johnston:

Let's Go Somewhere

Stumped for a Tale

Armchair Cricket

All About Cricket

It's Been a Lot of Fun

It's a Funny Game

Rain Stops Play

Chatterboxes

Now Here's a Funny Thing

It's Been a Piece of Cake

The Tale of Billy Bouncer

Down Your Way

FORTY-FIVE SUMMERS

Personal Memories of 264 Test Matches
Seen from the Commentary Box

by

Brian Johnston

PELHAM BOOKS

LONDON

Dedication

This pictorial account, of the 264 Test matches on which I have commentated to date on either TV or radio, is dedicated to all those many Test cricketers whom I have been proud to call my friends.

PELHAM BOOKS

Published by the Penguin Group
27 Wrights Lane, London W8 5TZ, England
Viking Penguin, a division of Penguin Books USA Inc
375 Hudson Street, New York, NY 10014, USA
Penguin Books Australia Ltd, Ringwood, Victoria, Australia
Penguin Books Canada Ltd, 2801 John Street, Markham, Ontario, Canada L3R 1B4
Penguin Books (NZ) Ltd, 182–190 Wairau Road, Auckland 10, New Zealand
Penguin Books Ltd, Registered Offices: Harmondsworth, Middlesex, England

First Published 1991
1 3 5 7 9 10 8 6 4 2
Text Copyright © Brian Johnston, 1991

Made and printed in Great Britain by
Butler & Tanner Ltd., Frome
Typeset by Goodfellow & Egan Ltd., Cambridge
Computer page make-up and design by Penny Mills

A CIP catalogue record for this book is available from the British Library.

ISBN 0 7207 1987 9

Hulton Picture Company, pp: 7(top left), 7(bottom left), 9, 10, 12(left), 12(right), 13, 14(top), 14(bottom), 15(top), 15(bottom), 16, 18(top right), 18(bottom left), 21(right), 22(left), 22(right), 24, 27(top right), 30, 32, 33(top), 33(middle), 34(bottom left), 40, 42(top), 42(bottom), 44, 45(top), 46/47(bottom), 47(right), 49(left), 49(right), 53(bottom), 54(bottom), 62(right), 64, 65, 66(bottom), 67, 68, 69, 70(left), 70(right), 72(top left), 73(left), 76, 82(top left), 83, 86, 87, 90, 92(top left), 92(bottom), 93(top), 94, 97, 101, 103, 108, 109, 124(bottom right). **Central Press**, pp: 35, 37(top right), 46(top), 75(bottom), 82(bottom), 93(bottom right), 127. **Keystone**, pp: 45(bottom), 72(bottom), 123(right). **Sport & General**, pp: 7(middle right), 19(top), 20, 23, 25(right), 28(right), 28(left), 29, 34(top right), 38, 39(bottom), 41, 50(top left), 50(bottom right), 51(bottom left), 52, 53(top), 55, 57(top), 57(bottom), 58, 59, 60(bottom), 61, 62(left), 74, 75(top), 77(top), 77(bottom), 85, 91. **Portman Press Bureau**, p: 11. **Ken Kelly**, pp: 27(bottom left), 37(bottom right), 43, 48(right), 51(top right), 81, 88, 95, 121, 147. **Yorkshire Post**, p: 27(bottom right). **Syndication**, p: 63(top right). **Patrick Eagar**, pp: 96, 98, 99, 100, 102, 104(left), 104(right), 105, 106, 107, 110(top right), 110(bottom), 111, 112, 113(top), 113(bottom left), 114, 115, 116, 117, 118(right), 118(left), 119, 120(top), 120(bottom), 122, 123(left), 124(top left), 124(top right), 125(top right), 125(bottom left), 126, 128, 129, 130(top right), 130(bottom), 131, 132, 133, 134(top right) 134(bottom left), 135(top left), 136(top right), 137, 138, 139, 140(top left), 140(bottom right), 141(top left), 141(top right), 141(bottom right), 142, 144, 145, 146, 148(top left), 148(bottom), 149, 150(top left), 150(bottom), 151, 152(top right), 152(bottom), 153, 154(left), 154(right), 155(top left), 155(bottom), 157(top left), 157(bottom), 159, 160, 161(top left), 161(top middle), 161(top right), 161(bottom right), 162(top), 162(bottom), 163(top), 163(bottom), 164, 165(middle left), 166, 167(top), 167(bottom right), 168, 169(top left), 169(top right), 169(bottom left), 170, 171(middle left), 171(middle right), 171(bottom middle), 172, 173(top left), 173(top right), 174(top left), 174(top right), 175(top left), 175(bottom right), 176. **Manchester Evening News**, pp: 135(bottom right). **Allsport**, pp: 89 (bottom left), 143. **Rex Features**, p:157(middle right). **David Munden**, p:165(top). **David Frith**, p:6. **The Photosource Ltd**, pp: 17, 19(bottom). **Press Association**, pp: 21(left) 158(middle right). **Pauline Johnston**, pp: 79, 80. **Brian Johnston's private collection** pp: 56, 69, 89(top), 158(top).

Every effort has been made to trace copyright owners but if there have been any omissions in this respect we apologise and will be pleased to make appropriate acknowledgement in any further editions.

INTRODUCTION

This book is a collection of pictorial memories from my 45 summers in the commentary box, either for television or radio, during the period 1946–1990.

Except for one or two personal occasions, the pictures refer only to Test Matches at home or abroad at which I have been present *as a commentator*.

From 1946 to 1966 I worked exclusively for television, and so missed 13 Tests from 1946 to 1952 when the BBC could only cover Lord's and The Oval. In 1950 the Sutton Coldfield transmitter opened up and Trent Bridge and Edgbaston came within range. Two years later the Holme Moss transmitter went into action and we were able to cover Headingley and Old Trafford to complete the six Test Match grounds.

Between 1958 and 1971 I commentated on 37 Tests abroad in all the Test Match playing countries except India. Since I retired as the BBC Cricket Correspondent in 1972, I have only commentated on one overseas Test – in 1983 at Sydney.

Of course much of my time in the 45 summers has been taken up with commentary on the County Championship and the various one-day internationals and one-day competitions. But to include all these would have meant a massive book, impossible to handle and a publisher's nightmare.

However I hope that many of you will be able to share in all or some of my Test memories, of what – to me – have been 45 summers of cricket, fun and happiness.

My special thanks are due to Ann Nash for typing the manuscript so beautifully, to Nick Yapp for all his expertise and research with the photographs, and to the 'Bearded Wonder' Bill Frindall for so kindly checking all the facts and figures (which are correct up to the end of 1990) to make sure I have not made any of my usual boobs.

Brian Johnston

St John's Wood
London
31 December 1990

1946

What better way to start a pictorial book of cricket memories than with this classical cover drive by Wally Hammond taken at Sydney in 1928. Note that as usual, his dark blue silk handkerchief is sticking out of his trouser pocket. In 1946 he was captaining England against India at Lord's in the first Test Match played since the war. It was also his last appearance in a Lord's Test Match. In spite of the seven years' lay-off he still maintained his old majesty and brilliance of stroke play, and indeed topped the season's first class batting averages with these amazing figures:

Inn.	Runs	H.S.	Av.	100s
26	1783	214	84·90	7

This was also Alec Bedser's first Test in his twenty-eighth year (left), and surprisingly his first regular first-class season – a late start due to the war. He took 11 wickets in the match. Alec proved too much for the Indian batsmen with his accurate in-swing bowling, bringing back memories of Maurice Tate with the way he made the ball zip off the pitch, thanks to his perfect swivel action.

A real treat to enjoy was a superb 205 not out by Joe Hardstaff (right), one of the most graceful and elegant stroke players I have seen, somewhat similar to Cyril Walters and Tom Graveney.

This Lord's Test was also the first Test to be televised since the war and so was the first of my Tests at the microphone for either TV or radio. One of my summarisers was Percy Fender (left). His nose was as large as mine, but his voice somewhat quieter. An engineer asked him to speak much closer to the mike: 'Hold it so that it touches your nose.' Percy retorted that it was already touching his nose!

1947

Those of us lucky enough to see this golden summer will never forget it. The sun shone, the crowds flocked to the grounds, and Bill Edrich and Denis Compton matched the sunshine with the brilliance of their batting. I'm not a great one for figures but the following does show their complete dominance over everyone against whom they played, including the tourists, South Africa.

	Inn.	N.O.	Runs	H.S.	Av.	100s
Compton	50	8	3816	246	90·85	18
Edrich	52	8	3539	267*	80·43	12

There was a complete contrast in their style of play, and in their characters.

Bill (below) was strong, sturdy, gutsy and determined. He had been a brave wartime bomber pilot, and showed immense courage which earned him the D.F.C. He was a great cutter, fearless hooker and scored many of his runs with a lofted pull shot between mid-wicket and mid-on. Not pretty to watch. But what a man to have on your side.

Denis was handsome, casual, forgetful, devil-may-care. A cavalier of cricket with dancing feet, unorthodox in attack, but strictly orthodox in defence. He was the supreme entertainer, and during his best years when he was fit, gave more pleasure to more people than any other cricketer I ever saw. (Opposite: Edrich and Compton at The Oval, 1947).

Had it not been for his knees, injured when playing football for the Arsenal, he would have gone on longer and splashed the pages of cricket history with even more brilliant performances. I remember especially his delicate late cut or chop, the drive square of cover just backward of point, his strong on-side play with his famous sweep (above). Those who played with him will recall that he was not the best judge of a run!

At the end of the 1947 season I went to see the Champion County v. the Rest of England at The Oval. (Middlesex were the champions winning 19 out of their 26 matches and finishing 20 points ahead of Gloucestershire in the Championship Table.) Denis's knee was playing him up. It was heavily strapped, and he had to retire hurt in the middle of his innings. But he came back and went on to make his eighteenth century and highest score of the season – 246. On one occasion as the bowler bowled, Denis's knee gave way and he fell over. Lying on the ground, he waited and swept the ball for 4 down to long leg. What a way to finish a season in which he passed Jack Hobbs's record number of centuries in a season (16) and Tom Haywards's record number of runs (3518).

An especially memorable year in which I got engaged and married to my wife, Pauline, all within the space of three months! A somewhat hectic start to an innings but – touch wood – we are still 42 not out. The BBC Outside Broadcasts Department did us the honours outside St Paul's, Knightsbridge, with an archway of microphones. We also set up house in leafy St John's Wood, where we have been ever since.

1948

The Australian Team of 1948 (opposite, arriving at Tilbury) *was undoubtedly the best ever to visit this country, and 1948 featured:*

1. Don Bradman's farewell to Test cricket.

2. Nineteen-year-old Neil Harvey's hundred in his first Test against England at Headingley (below, left).

3. The largely unsung opening left-hander Arthur Morris (below, right) *who averaged 87 in the five Tests.*

4. The fearsome and devastating fast bowling partnership of Ray Lindwall and Keith Miller. Ray was, I am sure, the better bowler, but the England batsmen preferred to play him rather than Keith.

1948

1 W Ferguson (scorer)
2 E R H Toshack
3 Sir Donald Bradman
4 S Loxton
5 D Ring
6 K R Miller
7 A L Hassett
8 W A Johnston
9 I W Johnson
10 D Tallon
11 K O E Johnson
   (Manager)
12 A R Morris
13 S G Barnes
14 R Saggers
15 W A Brown
16 R Hamence
17 R N Harvey
18 C L McCool

1948

Right: Lindwall in action. Below: Miller catches Yardley. Both pictures taken at The Oval, final Test, 1948.

England were completely outplayed and lost the series 0–4, but Denis Compton produced two courageous innings. He made 184 at Trent Bridge before treading on his wicket trying to avoid a bouncer (above), and 145 not out at Old Trafford when he pluckily came back after being cut over the eye by Lindwall (left).

Alec Bedser toiled away without much support and took 18 wickets in the series including Bradman's four times, three of which were caught by Len Hutton at backward short leg off inswingers, and the other caught by Edrich at slip off a fast leg-break.

The most dramatic moment of the tour was Don Bradman's final Test innings at The Oval. England batted first and against Lindwall at his best (6 for 20), collapsed, and were all out for 52. No one reached double figures except Hutton who was last out for 30, falling to a marvellous falling leg side catch by Don Tallon off Lindwall — Tallon holding the ball in his outstretched left hand.

Bradman came in to bat at 6 pm with Australia's reply at 117 for 1. He only needed 4 runs to take his Test aggregate to 7000, and his Test average to exactly 100. He was cheered all the way to the wicket by the capacity crowd, all standing. It was the most dramatic moment we had so far captured on TV, reminding you that we could televise only from Lord's and The Oval until 1950. When he approached the square Norman Yardley called for three cheers from his England team assembled together on the pitch (above).

I have asked Don two questions on several occasions:

1. 'Did this wonderful reception affect him emotionally so that he had perhaps a few tears in his eyes?' He has answered each time with an emphatic 'No'.

2. 'Did he know that he needed only 4 runs to reach 7000 and average 100?' To this he has replied with a chuckle: 'No, but if I had have known, I might have been a bit more careful!'

Anyway, what happened next is history. Eric Hollies was bowling his leg spin from the Vauxhall End. Don played his first ball quietly on the off side. To the second he stretched forward to what turned out to be Hollies's googly, and was bowled, possibly off the inside edge of his bat (below). There was a stunned silence as he turned slowly back towards the pavilion. The crowd then gave him an even bigger ovation than before. It was an emotional TV picture which showed him disappearing into the pavilion. The greatest run-getter ever in first class cricket had played in his last Test innings.

There is one interesting point about his dismissal. I was asked to do the commentary in a film of the match, and it showed Hollies bowling round the wicket. I am sure from what I saw personally, and I have checked with people like Hutton and Bedser, that he was bowling over the wicket as he usually did. The film makers probably only had Bradman in their shot and needed to show Hollies. They must have gone through the files to find a shot of Hollies bowling, and by bad luck chose one of him bowling round the wicket on some rare occasion.

1949

This is a good year in which to praise two of England's gutsiest performers, who were both all-rounders and played first-class cricket from 1949–1986, and from 1945–1967: Brian Close and Trevor Bailey.

Close (right) *became the youngest cricketer ever to represent England when at the age of eighteen he played against New Zealand in the third Test at Old Trafford. He made 0 (so did Len Hutton in his first Test innings) and was dropped from the last Test. But in this, his first season in first-class cricket, he unbelievably did the double with 1098 runs and 113 wickets. This influenced his selection for Freddie Brown's Australian tour of 1950–51 when, sad to relate, in the first and only Test in which he played, Close made 0 and 1. Not a happy tour for him.*

Trevor Bailey (below) *was luckier. His double in 1949 was 1380 runs and 130 wickets, and he played in all the Tests against New Zealand, taking 16 wickets and making 219 runs in the four Tests.*

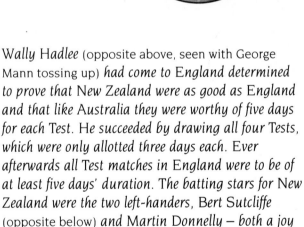

Wally Hadlee (opposite above, seen with George Mann tossing up) *had come to England determined to prove that New Zealand were as good as England and that like Australia they were worthy of five days for each Test. He succeeded by drawing all four Tests, which were only allotted three days each. Ever afterwards all Test matches in England were to be of at least five days' duration. The batting stars for New Zealand were the two left-handers, Bert Sutcliffe* (opposite below) *and Martin Donnelly – both a joy to watch.*

Donnelly made a fine 206 in the Lord's Test and so achieved a Lord's Treble of a hundred in the Varsity Match, in the Gents v. Players, and in a Test match, something which Percy Chapman had also achieved.

Hutton also made 206 at The Oval and had a successful series averaging 78. Compton also chipped in with two hundreds, and that model batsman, Jack Robertson, made a stylish 121 at Lord's only to be dropped for the next Test!

At Lord's we were sent scurrying to check our Laws and Regulations when George Mann declared England's first innings at 313 for 9, shortly before 6 pm on the first day. It proved to be illegal because the experimental law for first-class cricket which allowed first day declarations, did not apply to Test cricket. Luckily New Zealand did not lose a wicket that evening, so England gained no advantage.

1950

This was the year when West Indies cricket really came of age. They haven't looked back since. They won the series 3–1 and at Lord's in the second Test beat England for the first time ever in England. This was the famous Calypso Test when a soft hatted guitar player led a colourful happy crowd across the ground right up to the pavilion rails (above). They sang 'Cricket, Lovely Cricket' and although the MCC members had never seen anything like it, they overcame their surprise and entered into the carnival spirit.

Then the crowd sang 'Ramadhin' and 'Valentine'. And no wonder. These two twenty-year-old spinners had taken 11 and 7 wickets respectively in the match, and by the end of the series had taken 26 and 33 in only four Tests. It was a staggering performance, considering that before they came on tour they both had played only in two first-class matches. (A hint for our selectors?).

What a contrast they were. Ramadhin (opposite, above left) Sonny by name and nature, was about 5 feet 4 inches tall, a right-arm spinner who always bowled in a cap with his sleeves buttoned up at the wrist. He bowled mainly off-spin with an occasional very well disguised leg-break. None of the England batsmen could read him at first. Nor, or so we thought, did wicket-keeper Clyde Walcott. We noticed on TV that Sonny used sometimes to run his left hand down the back of his cap before he bowled. Whenever he did this a leg-break usually followed, so we suspected it was to help Walcott. Needless to say John Goddard, the West Indian captain, denied this when I interviewed him on TV.

But we also warned the England batsmen. Perhaps that was why Len Hutton played one of his great innings at The Oval, carrying his bat for 202 not out.

Alfred Valentine (above, right) *was taller, wore spectacles and had a cheerful toothy grin. He was an orthodox left-arm spinner who really gave the ball a tweak, after a run-up of only a few steps.*

1950

Nineteen fifty also introduced us to the three Ws — and what a combination they were! Frank Worrell (below left) *was the stylist,* Clyde Walcott (opposite) *the power driver off both front and back feet, and Everton Weekes* (below right) *the complete batsman with every stroke in the game. On the tour they all averaged over 55 and made 5759 runs between them, whilst in the Tests Worrell had scores of 261 and 138, Weekes 129, and Walcott 168 not out. They were to be the scourge of all Test bowlers for the next eight years or so.*

It was also an important year for BBC TV, as with the opening of the Sutton Coldfield transmitter we were able to televise a Test match from outside London for the first time. This was the third Test at Trent Bridge where Worrell and Weekes put on 283 for the fourth wicket. This unfortunately caused me to say on TV towards the end of the stand: 'This is an enormous problem for Norman Yardley. I wonder what he can do to stop the flow of runs. Let's get the camera on to him at mid-on.' It was bad luck that when we panned on to him he was scratching his private parts! I hastily added: 'It's obviously a very ticklish problem!' He got a terrific rocket from his wife, Toni, when he got home.

1951

South Africa were the visitors and lost the series 1–3. Peter May made his Test debut in the fourth Test at Headingley, celebrated it with a hundred, and so became the seventh England batsman to score a century in his first Test and the only one to do so against South Africa in England. Alas, I did not see it as the BBC were not able to televise from the north until 1952 when the Holme Moss transmitter was finally built.

Instead, I did a different sort of television commentary for Terence Rattigan's cricket play called The Final Test, which he wrote especially for the BBC in Festival of Britain year. It was later made into a film starring Robert Morley and Jack Warner, and included guest appearances by some of the England team including Bedser, Washbrook, Compton, Hutton, Laker and Evans (below). I think they found that cricket was rather easier than acting!

We were, though, able to televise the first Test at Trent Bridge when I saw one of the pluckiest innings ever. The South African captain, Dudley Nourse (left), went into the match with a fractured thumb, and though in great pain he stayed for nine hours ten minutes and made 208 before being run out. This was South Africa's first double century against England, but it was soon followed by another one in the fourth Test at Headingley where that dynamic character Eric Rowan (seen below in cap, with John Waite) made 236.

In the other two Tests on which I commentated, off-spinner Roy Tattersall took 12 wickets at Lord's on a rain affected pitch. He took 21 wickets in the series and, but for Jim Laker, could have played in more than 16 Tests.

At The Oval during the fifth Test we saw the only instance in Test cricket of a batsman being given out for obstruction: I wish we had had an action replay in those days, as it was the first time most people had ever seen it happen, and it was all over in a flash. What happened was that off-spinner Athol Rowan bowled a ball which bounced a bit and ballooned into the air off the top edge of Hutton's bat, or possibly off his glove. He thought it was going to fall on his stumps and so waved his bat at it, trying to fend it away. Actually he missed it, but by waving his bat he certainly obstructed the wicket-keeper Russell Endean from making what would have been a very easy catch (above).

Dai Davies was the umpire who gave him out, but I remember that Frank Chester, the other umpire, had to go over to the scorers to explain what had happened. Some people thought at the time that Hutton had hit the ball a second time, and so was out 'hitting the ball twice'. But this was wrong thinking because a batsman is allowed to hit the ball twice in an effort to prevent it hitting his wicket. But of course Hutton did unintentionally obstruct the wicket-keeper and so was rightly given out — a funny way to end his one hundredth Test innings.

A great year for TV. For the first time we were able to televise from Headingley and Old Trafford. It was also the first time that a professional – Len Hutton – had been appointed as captain of England, in England, though Jack Hobbs had taken over the captaincy for two days at Old Trafford in 1926, when A. W. Carr became ill with tonsillitis. (NB James Lillywhite, Alfred Shaw and Arthur Shrewsbury – all professionals – had captained England in Australia.)

Len Hutton seen right reading his many congratulatory telegrams.

And what a start it was for TV, Len – and Fred Trueman (left) making his first Test appearance at the age of 21. When India batted a second time, 41 runs behind England, they lost 4 wickets for no runs in the first 14 balls, Trueman getting 3 and Bedser 1. Young Fred bowled with tremendous pace and fire, and you can imagine the excitement in the commentary box. The scoreboard (below) read 0 for 4, the worst start ever by a Test team.

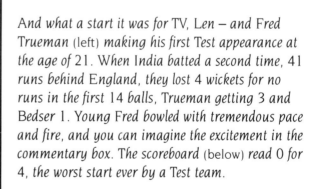

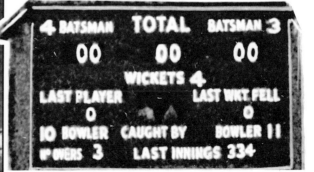

Fred took 7 wickets in this match, 8 at Lord's, 9 at Old Trafford and 5 in the only innings at The Oval. Twenty-nine wickets in his first Test series – the shape of things to come! But I must admit he owed a lot to the Indian batsmen, not used to such speed. They obviously did not relish it, and at Old Trafford especially, some of their batsmen came near to knocking over the square-leg umpire, in their hasty retreat.

The second Test at Lord's was a good one for Godfrey Evans (below left). He became the first England wicket-keeper to make a hundred dismissals in Tests. He also made 98 in the session before lunch on the third day with some swashbuckling strokes, and cheeky running between the wickets, including a five, all run up to the clock at the nursery end.

There was also an incredible all-round performance by Vinoo Mankad (right), especially released for the match by Haslingden in the Lancashire League where he was their professional.

He showed remarkable endurance and staying power. He not only made 72 and 184 when opening the batting but also bowled 97 overs in the match taking 5 wickets. I wonder what the Queen said to him when he was presented to her, on her first visit to Lord's since she became Queen (above).

This was also the year when I received a rather unexpected answer to a question I put to the Indian Manager, Mr Gupte, during a TV interview in their first match at Worcester. It was during a long stoppage for rain, and I was asking him about his team. He replied that they had seven very good batsmen, and six very good bowlers. I then asked him, 'what about yourself? Are you a selector?' 'No,' he replied, 'I'm a Christian!'

1953

What a year! The Coronation; Gordon Richards won his first and only Derby on Pinza and was knighted; Stanley Matthews received his long-awaited FA Cup-winners medal; and England regained the Ashes after 19 years. TV covered all five Australian Tests for the first time, and what value we got.

There were Alec Bedser's 14 wickets in the first Test at Trent Bridge (below), where he bowled magnificently, and passed Sydney Barnes's record of 189 wickets for England. The grand old man, tall, erect and straight-backed at the age of 80, was there to see it and congratulate him. There was an amusing incident one evening during Australia's second innings when they were struggling against Bedser and Tattersall. Don Tallon, the Australian wicket-keeper, was due to go in, and with the score at 81 for 6 dour defence was obviously needed. As he left the dressing-room Lindsay Hassett, the Australian captain, shouted after him, 'Deafy, give the light a go,' – meaning to appeal against the light. As you will have gathered Tallon was deaf and thinking his captain had said 'Have a go' he proceeded to attack the bowling and make a quick 15 before being caught by Reg Simpson going for a big hit off Tattersall. At the time we were puzzled at his unusual tactics, and even our summarisers Jack Fingleton and Jim Swanton could not think of an explanation.

In the second Test at Lord's there was a thrilling last day with England who had lost Hutton, Graveney and Kenyon for 12 runs, and then at 73 Compton was out for a fighting 33. This brought Trevor Bailey (above left) and Willie Watson (above right) together and for the next four hours eight minutes we watched a grim rearguard action. They put on 163 for the fifth wicket and saved the day for England. The game was watched by huge crowds, the aggregate attendance being 137,915, an average of about 27,000 a day. Our house was only 80 yards from the ground and I remember waking up to the sound of the giant queue which completely encircled Lord's. I believe at least 10,000 were shut out on one day. These figures would not be possible today, as there are now seats in front of the Tavern, and no one is allowed to sit on the grass as they did then.

After four draws the climax came at The Oval, where I was lucky to be the commentator at the moment England regained the Ashes on the last afternoon. With England cruising to victory Hassett gave himself one over and then brought on Arthur Morris with his left-arm chinamen from the Pavilion End. Edrich and Compton had put on 39 together and five runs were still needed for victory.

1953

Edrich scored a single and then off Morris's fourth ball Compton made one of his famous sweeps. The crowd, already mustered in their starting-blocks all round the ground, thought it was a certain four. So did we. They rushed on to the ground but they had reckoned without the giant claw of Alan Davidson at backward short leg, who somehow managed to stop the ball. There was a tense delay as the crowds were ushered back behind the boundary line. Then Morris bowled again, an off-break outside the leg stump — just the ball for another Compton sweep. He swept it past the short legs (top) and the crowd erupted. Whether the ball ever got to the boundary down by the gasholders we shall never know. (Perhaps the lucky person who picked up the ball, and probably still has it, could tell us!)

The subsequent scenes made wonderful television as the players led by Edrich and Compton with bats held aloft squeezed their way through the crowd back to the pavilion (above).

There were speeches to the massed crowd by Len Hutton and Lindsay Hassett from the balcony (opposite), and there were scenes of great jubilation everywhere, especially in the dressing rooms, where the clock got the worst of the argument with a flung bottle of champagne.

It was my most exciting moment on television and I have often listened to a recording of my voice, hoarse with emotion, shouting: 'It's the Ashes, it's the Ashes.'

1954

I always recall 1954 as having grandmother weather – wet and windy. It was also Pakistan's first tour here and, by a sensational win at The Oval in the fourth and last Test, they drew the series. (Opposite page: A.H. Kadar acknowledges the cheers of the crowd.) It was a great triumph for them, though the England selectors made it easier by leaving out Bailey and Bedser, so as to give Loader and Tyson a trial.

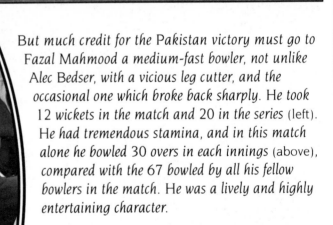

But much credit for the Pakistan victory must go to Fazal Mahmood a medium-fast bowler, not unlike Alec Bedser, with a vicious leg cutter, and the occasional one which broke back sharply. He took 12 wickets in the match and 20 in the series (left). He had tremendous stamina, and in this match alone he bowled 30 overs in each innings (above), compared with the 67 bowled by all his fellow bowlers in the match. He was a lively and highly entertaining character.

In this Oval Test, Godfrey Evans passed Bertie Oldfield's record number of 130 Test victims for a wicket-keeper. Because Bailey had been left out Godfrey had to bat at No. 6 – about two places too high. He made 3 in the second innings, and was 3 runs less successful in the first!

Whenever I go to Trent Bridge I am reminded of one of Compton's most brilliant innings – 278, his highest score in Test cricket. We were convinced on TV that, once he had reached his hundred, he was trying to get out. He played every stroke in the book, and many that are not in it. Dancing down the pitch he peppered the field with outrageous unorthodoxy and in a stand of 192 with Trevor Bailey actually made 165 of them in 105 minutes with a six and 33 fours. Fantastic entertainment.

1955

This summer of glorious sunshine saw the retirement of Len Hutton and Alec Bedser from Test cricket, and the start of Peter May's record of captaining England 41 times. It also produced one of the best and closest Test series of any which I have seen. South Africa lost the first two Tests, won the next two but lost the final one at The Oval.

Under the captaincy of Jack Cheetham (seen below when I interviewed him for the BBC) *they were the best fielding side ever to come to England. They set up a new standard by chasing and throwing themselves at the ball, in order to save a boundary. This made off-spinner 'Toey' Tayfield* (opposite, above) *particularly difficult to score off and enabled him to take 26 wickets. He was very accurate and used to set a strong off-side field, plus, unusually, two mid-ons alongside each other.*

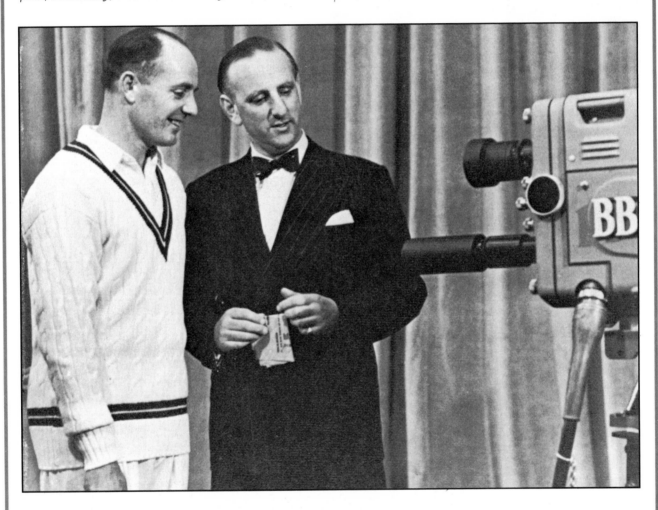

The best and most exciting Test was the third at Old Trafford with the fortunes of each side swinging backwards and forwards. South Africa finally won by 3 wickets with nine balls to spare. You can't ask for anything closer than that over five days.

It was Alec Bedser's last Test, and Godfrey Evans also fractured the little finger of his right hand trying to take one of Frank Tyson's expresses. Frank (below) had just returned from his great success in Australia but due to injuries only played in two Tests. Even so he took 14 wickets, and with his terrifying speed we could understand why he had been such a terror on the faster Australian pitches.

1955

Someone had to take Godfrey's place and there wasn't too much competition! But as Tom Graveney explains, 'I had made 0 and 1 and dropped a couple of slip catches so I was the team's most popular choice!' The first ball of Tyson's which he tried to take broke the little finger of his left hand — it's still crooked today!

In the 1945 Victory Test at Lord's, Keith Miller had nearly hit Rex Alston in the radio commentary box above the England dressing-room. It was a giant six right up to the top balcony. In 1955 at Old Trafford, Paul Winslow made an even more dramatic hit. In those days, the TV commentators were perched on a scaffold about 60 feet above the ground looking down over long-on. It was a popular sight for spectators to watch the ample figures of Roy Webber and Jim Swanton climb up the more or less vertical ladder. Roy, I know, used to stay there all day, in spite of the call of nature. He wasn't going to risk two climbs in one day.

Tony Lock was bowling to Paul Winslow (left) from the Stretford End where we were. Paul was on 94 and had never made a first-class century. Lock tossed him up a half volley and Paul drove it high over the sightscreen, just missing a terrified waffle of TV commentators as it sailed past our box. It was a terrific six and a good way to reach one's maiden century.

In this match the South African fast bowlers showed what a formidable combination they made picking up 14 wickets between them in the match, with some unpleasantly hostile bowling. It didn't worry Denis Compton who played another of his out-of-character Test innings demanded by the situation. He made 158 but it took him five and a half hours.

Jim Laker was the only cricketer I knew to have had a year named after him, until Botham in 1981. In cricket circles 1956 is simply known as Laker's year. His bowling figures against the Australians during the summer were unbelievable. Ten for 88 in their first innings against Surrey; then 19 for 90 in the Old Trafford Test. He took 46 wickets in the series, and picked up another 5 Australian wickets when they played Surrey a second time immediately following Old Trafford. This brought his total of Australian wickets during the summer to 63.

Jim was the perfect off-spinner, probably the best that there has ever been. He had a high action from which he got bounce, a fine swivel action, prodigious spin (you should have seen the size and shape of his spinning figure) and a well-disguised away-floater.

What impressed me most about his Old Trafford performance was the calm modest way in which he took his triumph. No histrionics, no kissing, no punching of the air, no hugging. He just quietly took his sweater from umpire Frank Lee and trudged slowly back to the pavilion with that measured tread of his, a slow smile acknowledging the acclaim of the crowd, and the look of disbelief on the faces of his team mates (right).

Below: the Laker leg trap strikes, Burke caught Lock, Old Trafford, 1956

I went across to get him for a TV interview and found him sitting quietly in the corner of the dressing-room, whilst the champagne corks flew all round him. He had a long drive back to London – Surrey were playing the Australians next day. On his way he stopped at a pub, and quite unrecognised, quietly watched the repeat of his feat on TV.

I cannot believe that his 19 for 90 will ever be equalled, let alone beaten. It was made even more remarkable by the fact that Tony Lock – on a pitch on which England had made 459, but which began to take spin after the first two days – bowling from the Warwick Road end, bowled more overs in the match than Laker (69 against 68). Yet, try as he could he only took 1 for 106. In desperation he began to bowl faster and faster. Perhaps he tried too hard.

Nineteen fifty-six was also the selectors' year under the chairmanship of Gubby Allen. They couldn't put a foot wrong. They kept roughly the same team together through the series but added the occasional sweetener. They brought back Washbrook (seen opposite walking out with Peter May) at Headingley. He had not played in a Test since 1951 but after surviving a hair-raising appeal for lbw before he had scored, went on to make 98. At Old Trafford they selected the Rev David Sheppard after a two year gap from Test cricket and he made 113, and to (knee) cap it all at The Oval they recalled Denis Compton. He had missed half the season recovering from an operation to remove his right kneecap. He didn't seem to miss it as he made 94 and 35 not out. Not a bad hat trick for the selectors. I was pretty unpopular with Denis's wife, Valerie, as I had just said on TV what a great performance it would be if – as he was on 94 – he could hit a six to get his hundred. The very next ball he turned into the massive hands of Alan Davidson at backward short leg.

Oh, by the way, there was a most unusual occurrence before the start of the Old Trafford Test. During the night before, Gil Langley (left), the Australian wicket-keeper, slept on his hand, and so damaged it that he could not play, and Len Maddocks took his place.

1957

The number 411 always reminds me of the first Test at Edgbaston in 1957. It was the match saving stand for the 4th wicket between Peter May (285 not out) and Colin Cowdrey (154). They came together at 11.50 am on Monday when England, batting again, had lost 3 wickets for 113 runs. This is still the highest 4th wicket partnership in all Test cricket, and the highest for England for any wicket.

Press, commentators and even the players were all caught out and had booked out of their hotels over the weekend, not thinking that England could possibly last the whole of the Monday. As it was, May and Cowdrey batted together until 2.50 pm on the Tuesday.

In England's first innings Ramadhin (below, bowling to Cowdrey) *had run amok amongst the England batsmen taking 7 for 49 in their total of 186. West Indies replied with 474 thanks largely to Walcott (90), Worrell (81) and a brilliant 161 by Collie Smith (left), who also made 168 in the third Test. He was an exuberant character who loved cricket and played it with obvious enjoyment. He was one of the most popular cricketers ever to come from the West Indies, and it was tragic that he was killed in a motor accident two years later.*

But to get back to Ramadhin. England's second innings, after he had taken the first 2 wickets, was to be his death sentence. Frank Worrell was injured and could not bowl. So Ramadhin had to bowl 98 overs, of which 35 were maidens, and he took 2 for 179. It was a tremendous feat of endurance, as he wheeled away, hour after hour. His 588 balls in the second innings is still a record number for any first-class innings, and his grand total of balls delivered in the match – 774 – is still the record for any Test. He was never the same again. His confidence was undermined and in the remaining four Tests he took only 5 more wickets.

The May–Cowdrey stand was a great fight back but was not very edifying to watch. They countered Ramadhin by playing forward, frequently using their pads as the first line of defence. We lost count of the number of appeals for lbw turned down by the umpires Emrys Davies and Frank Lee. Cowdrey had worked out this method of playing Ramadhin's off-spin to perfection. His judgement of line was spot-on. He just went on and on prodding forward with bat and pad together. His hundred took him seven and three-quarter hours, but his next fifty came in 55 minutes.

May (above) was much freer and played some delightful strokes, many of his 25 fours coming from drives through the covers. Thanks to him and his declaration there was a most exciting finish, West Indies quickly losing 7 wickets for only 72 runs before the match ended in a draw.

There are two points worth noting:-

1. In those days a batsman was not out if the part of his body hit by the ball was outside the line of the off stump. Today the batsman is out unless he has attempted to play a stroke at the ball. So all Cowdrey had to do was to make sure his left pad which the ball hit was outside the off stump. He would not have got away with it today.

2. The 'destruction' of Ramadhin affected the result of the whole series which England won 3–0.

Nineteen fifty-seven was a good year for Tom Graveney (below). He hadn't played at Edgbaston but replaced Doug Insole at Lord's, where he promptly made 0. However he made up for it at Trent Bridge and The Oval when he made 258 and 164, and brought a touch of grace and elegant stroke play to the tough and sometimes dour Test Match scene.

New Zealand were only a moderate side and England under Peter May won the first four Tests easily, and looked like winning the last one except that rain prevented more than 12 hours' play. Throughout the summer, the New Zealand batsmen were quite unable to cope with the spin of Lock (left) and Laker, Lock taking 34 wickets in the series, and Laker 17. The Oval produced a highlight for Freddie Trueman (below). He made 39 not out which included three giant sixes and was his highest score in Test Matches. It has given him something to boast about ever since!

It was during the summer that I discovered that after ten years with the BBC I was entitled to something called 'grace leave'. This meant I could take three months off with pay. I had never seen a Test Match overseas so, to improve my cricket education, I decided to go to Australia to see the last four Tests of Peter May's tour.

1958-59

Australia

They were heralded as the strongest side ever to leave these shores, but a mixture of injuries and an epidemic of throwing by the Australian bowlers meant that they lost the series 1–4, and so Australia regained the Ashes.

I arrived for the second Test at Melbourne after Australia had won the Brisbane Test by 8 wickets in spite of a more than typical rear-guard action by Trevor Bailey. He made 68 in seven hours 18 minutes, including 50 in 357 minutes – still the slowest fifty in all first-class cricket. He ended the tour on a sad note, making a pair at Melbourne, going in first in what was his last Test.

The ABC (the BBC of Australia) had kindly included me in their radio commentary team, but I got off to an inauspicious start. Only 24 hours earlier I had flown in on a Britannia after a 48-hour flight, with two rest stops on the way. Due to Alan McGilvray's internal flight being late I was flung right in at the deep end, and was the second commentator to broadcast. When I took over after only 20 minutes' play, England, after winning the toss were 7 for 3, Alan Davidson (above right) dismissing Peter Richardson, Willie Watson and Tom Graveney with the first, fourth and fifth balls of his second over.

Richardson made 3, the other two 0. To make matters worse, as I took my seat in the vast Members' Stand, a pigeon dropped a message of welcome on to my wrist.

No wickets fell in my second spell an hour later, thanks to a gallant stand of 85 between Peter May and Trevor Bailey.

England were outplayed by Australia, skilfully captained by Richie Benaud in his first series as captain. His leg-breaks also puzzled our batsmen, and he took 31 wickets in the series, at a cost of only 18.83. He was well supported by the fast left-arm bowling of Alan Davidson who took 24 wickets.

The throwing accusations slightly soured the atmosphere but there was no doubt that Meckiff (below), Slater, Burke and the giant Rorke (right) were all guilty. In addition Rorke bowled from only 18 yards, so long was his drag.

But in spite of England's defeat, my first tour was an enjoyable experience, getting to know Australia and making many friends whom I still see to this day. I was also to learn at first hand the great difference between Australian and English broadcasting techniques. The most obvious difference is their way of putting the wickets which have fallen before the score, for example at Melbourne when I said England were 7 for 3, they said 3 for 7. They used to say sundries instead of extras, but they have now reverted to extras. But 'Close of Play' is still definitely 'Stumps'.

1959

This was a beautiful summer with England making a clean sweep of all five Tests against India – the first time they had ever done this against any country.

Colin Cowdrey (left) captained England for the first time in the last two Tests as Peter May had to have an operation, breaking his sequence of 52 consecutive appearances for England (equalling the record at that time held by Frank Woolley), 35 of them as captain.

Colin came in for a bit of criticism by announcing in advance, before play started on the third day, that for the sake of the spectators and because there was a good weather forecast, he would not enforce the follow on, so ensuring play on the Bank Holiday Monday.

I remember reading an item tucked away at the bottom of a sports page. It reported that a well-built 17-year-old had made a sparkling hundred for Durham against the Indians. His name was Colin Milburn (right). The shape of things to come!

*E*ngland had another successful season, winning the first three Tests against South Africa, the other two being drawn. Best performances came from those old crusaders Brian Statham (below left) and Freddie Trueman with their contrasting styles. They took 27 and 25 wickets respectively.

In batting, another partnership who in the previous winter had opened together in all five Tests against West Indies – Colin Cowdrey and Geoff Pullar – put on 290 for the 1st wicket in England's second innings at The Oval. This match ended in a rather boring draw and we were finding it difficult to entertain the viewers.

So, to liven things up, we sent out a telegram to Neil Adcock (below right). Inside it was, I'm ashamed to admit, a pornographic photograph. When he opened it he roared with laughter and looked up at our TV commentary box, as he suspected it could only have come from us. All the players – and the two umpires – surrounded him at the end of the over, and there was much laughter from everyone. Our colleagues on the radio knew nothing of our 'joke' and were making suggestions as to what the telegram had contained. 'Had Adcock won the pools?' 'Had his wife had twins?' – that sort of thing. When Adcock returned to the pavilion at lunch-time he had to give a press conference to try to explain to the media what was in the telegram. But he didn't give us away.

1960

The sensation of the season happened in the second Test at Lord's. Ever since England's 1958–59 tour of Australia the question of throwing had become cricket's biggest problem. All the countries, led by England, were trying to find a solution to solve it.

During the early summer, fast bowler Geoff Griffin had been no-balled for throwing 17 times, as South Africa toured round the country. At Lord's in England's only innings he was again no-balled, 11 times, by Frank Lee standing at square leg. The remarkable thing was that in between times Griffin did the hat trick, the first ever by a South African, and still the first in a Test at Lord's.

There was worse to come – a complete farce in fact. Because England won just after lunch on the fourth day, an exhibition match between the two teams was hurriedly arranged. During it, Griffin (below) only bowled one over consisting of 11 deliveries. Sid Buller called no-ball for four out of his first five balls. His captain Jackie McGlew then suggested to him that he should finish the over bowling underarm (left).

And believe it or not, after his first delivery he was no-balled by Frank Lee because Griffin had failed to warn the batsman that he was going to change from overarm to lobs! I have never seen a more extraordinary sequence of events in any Test Match.

Australia, under Richie Benaud, retained the Ashes by winning the series 2–1. Benaud was troubled with a bad right shoulder, but even so played a big part in Australia's victory with his charismatic and cunning captaincy, besides picking up 15 wickets in four Tests. The first Test at Edgbaston was drawn thanks to a typical Dexter innings of 180 (right), hitting 31 fours. Neil Harvey (seen below with Colin Cowdrey tossing up) captained Australia at Lord's in place of the injured Benaud and they won by 5 wickets. This was the only time that Harvey captained Australia so he has always boasted of his 100 per cent record.

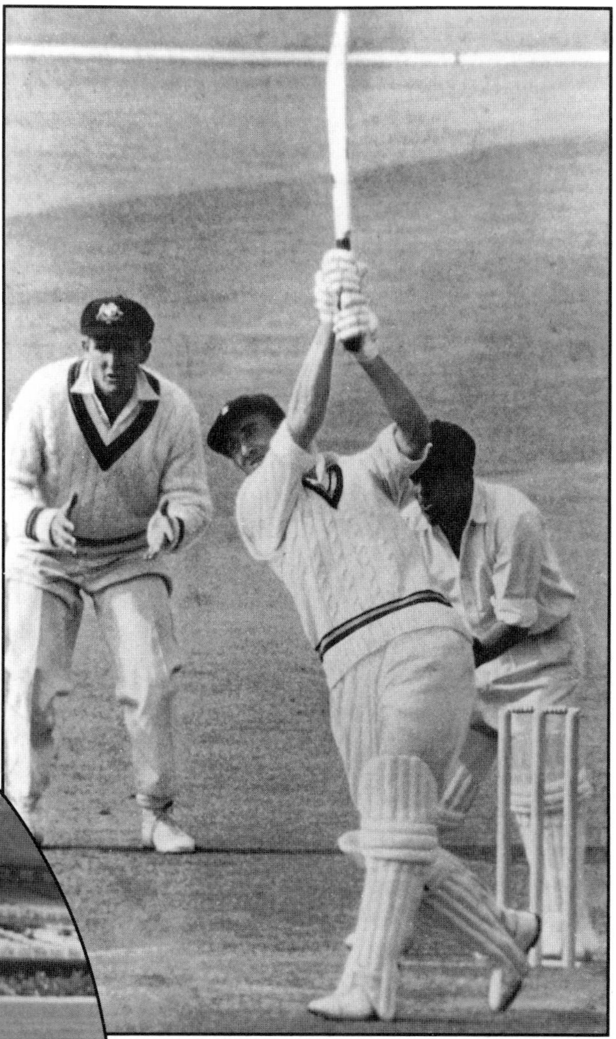

Alan Davidson bowled superbly in England's first innings, bowling fast left-arm over the wicket, slanting the ball across the batsmen, and then swinging the odd one in late into the batsmen, beautifully disguised.

1961

Davidson (above, in sweater and cap) *had a reputation of being a hypochondriac, and used to spend many happy hours on the massage table. He had hobbled off after taking the wicket of Geoff Pullar. Without Benaud, Australia were short of bowlers, so during the lunch interval Richie thought of a ploy to get Davo back on the pitch. He pleaded with Davo to get off the table and go out with the team after lunch. He knew Davo and Neil were close friends. 'Look, Davo,' he said, 'This is Neil's first time as captain. Won't you make a special effort to help him?' Davo lay there thinking for a moment or two, then leapt up and said: 'For the little fellow I'd do anything. For him anything I'd do.' He went out and with some devastating bowling promptly took 4 more wickets!*

The Australians were not too happy with the state of the Headingley pitch. (Not the first overseas team to complain there!) It was a greyish colour, having been overheated with chemicals, and the ball hopped about all over the place. Freddie Trueman took full advantage of this, and instead of bowling flat out bowled accurate off cutters and took 11 wickets to help win the match. He was well supported by the Derbyshire fast bowler, Les Jackson (opposite, above), *who played instead of Statham, who was injured. This was the second of only two Tests in which Jackson played, and yet he would have been a permanent member of the England team had his fellow professionals been selectors. A much underrated bowler.*

In mid-afternoon on the last day of the fourth Test at Old Trafford, Gubby Allen, in his seventh year as chairman of selectors, got into his Bentley to drive back to London. He was well satisfied with England's position. They were 150 for 1 needing just 106 more runs to win with about two hours left. Subba Row and Dexter were together, the latter driving and cutting with tremendous power. But Gubby then had the most miserable drive of his life.

Benaud, in spite of his injured shoulder never gave up, and suddenly decided to switch to round the wicket, and to bowl into the rough, on or just outside the leg stump at the other end. He started by telling Wally Grout behind the stumps that he was going to tempt Dexter by bowling short outside his off stump. Grout demurred and didn't think much of the idea. 'Stay with me Wal,' Benaud is reported as saying, and to Grout's surprise Dexter, attempting to force the ball away of the back foot, snicked it to Grout and was out for 76 (below).

1961

Benaud then bowled his rival captain Peter May round his legs for 0 (above). After playing a couple of dangerous looking cross bat strokes Close was caught round the corner. Immediately afterwards Subba Row was clean bowled by Benaud, and England's collapse was complete. They took tea, still needing 93 to win in 85 minutes. But they then lost their last 5 wickets for 38 runs and Australia had won by 54 runs with 20 minutes to spare. A great triumph for Benaud who took 6 for 70 including a spell of 5 for 12 in 25 balls. His decision to go round the wicket was a desperate measure, but it came off.

England's task would have been far easier but for a hard hitting last wicket partnership of 98 between Davidson and McKenzie. David Allen had been turning his off-breaks considerably, but Davidson suddenly hit him for 20 in one over. This prompted May to take off Allen immediately. With hindsight it was probably a mistake.

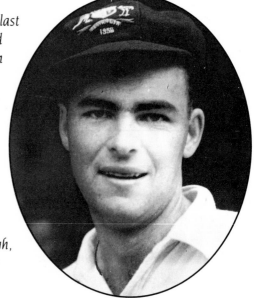

With the Oval Test drawn, Australia ended their tour by playing Ireland in Dublin where a good time was had by all! As the Australians left the field after beating Ireland, Peter Burge (right), who had made 181 at The Oval, took off his baggy green Australian cap and threw it to me as he passed our commentary box. A final and generous gesture by an old friend, and it's hanging behind me on the wall as I write. Funnily enough, though, it may not have been so generous after all – inside is the name C. McDonald!

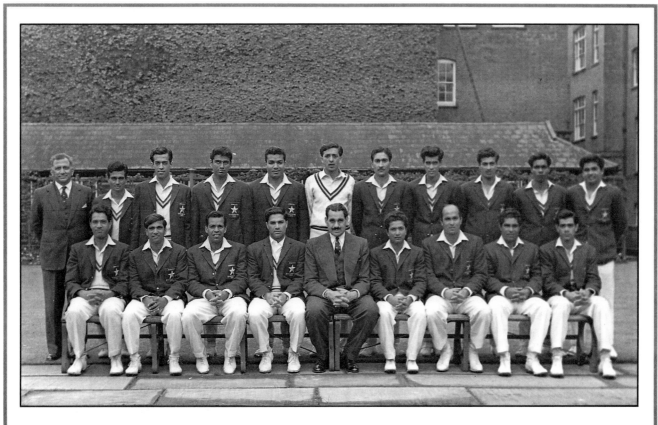

Ted Dexter took over the England captaincy from Peter May and made a successful start by beating Pakistan 4–0. Pakistan was not a very good side, and suffered badly from injuries. The England batsmen had a field day, seven of them averaging over 70, with eight hundreds between them.

The Pakistan manager was a delightful man called Brigadier Hyder (seen above with the team), very much a soldier of the old school. He was strong on discipline but lacking in knowledge of cricket. At Headingley, Pakistan was in desperate straits, and at one time had as many as three substitutes on the field. This didn't please the Brigadier who undoubtedly thought that they were all softies. One unfortunate bowler called Mohammed Farooq limped off the field with what later proved to be a double hernia. He was met at the steps of the pavilion by the Brigadier who waved him away and said: 'Go back on to the field and fight for Pakistan!' Again, in their second innings their cheerful opening bat Alimuddin was out for 60, having already made 50 in the first innings. He was having a well earned rest on the massage table, as Pakistan wickets were falling rapidly outside. The Brigadier spotted him, and in spite of Alim's explanation that he had already batted, told him to put on his pads and go out to fight for Pakistan, and stop the rot!

The Brigadier's assistant was Major Rahmann who was a very puzzled man when he came to play cricket for me one day. It was my annual match against the village of Widford in Hertfordshire. When we were fielding I thought I would experiment, and whenever a bowler had taken a wicket, I immediately took him off. By an amazing piece of luck it turned out that every member of the side each took one wicket, which must be unique in any class of cricket (see scorecard overleaf). But the Major, who had not realised what was happening, was slightly resentful when I took him off as soon as he had taken a wicket with the last ball of his second over.

1962

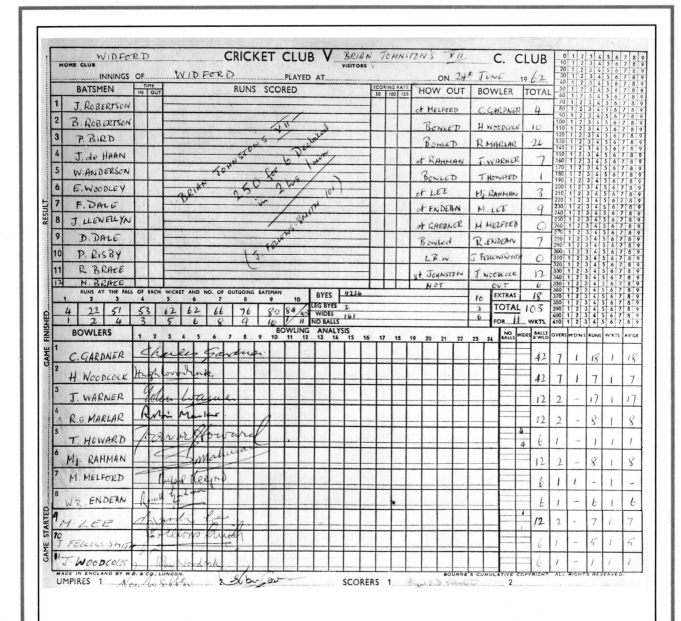

1962

One of the best gaffes ever made was perpetrated by Rex Alston in the Lord's Test. In the Pakistan team there was a bowler with the unfortunate name of Afaq Hussain (right). It was an anxious moment for all commentators when they checked to see if he was playing. When Pakistan came to Lord's to play MCC, I was on TV, Rex on the radio. I hastily examined my score-card and to my relief saw that Afaq had not been selected. I rushed into the radio box and said to Rex: 'It's jolly lucky this chap Afaq is not playing.' He replied: 'Don't say his name again or I shall get it into my head.' So, murmuring Afaq, Afaq, Afaq I left the box. I am assured by Rex's fellow commentator, Alan Gibson, that at five o'clock MCC were something like 250 for 6 with Barry Knight of Essex about 37 not out. Rex then said: 'Now for something different. We are going to see Afaq to Knight at the nursery end.' If you say it out loud you will see why everyone in the box was helpless with laughter. It was made even worse when Rex clutched his head and said: 'What am I saying? He's not even playing!'

Nineteen sixty-two was the year when the last of 137 Gentlemen v. Players matches was played. The amateur disappeared from first-class cricket and everyone became a paid cricketer. It was a sad loss to cricket. The amateur had brought a spirit of fun and adventure into the game and as captains they were not too close to the other players, which made discipline and selection much easier.

Left: Fred Trueman leading out the Players

Australia

I went on my second tour of Australia, for the BBC, to cover what proved to be a rather disappointing drawn series. Both Ted Dexter and Richie Benaud were by nature attacking cricketers and captains, but sadly they both used safety-first tactics in the last two Tests. There were one or two bright spots. For England, Ken Barrington had a great series averaging 72.75 in the Tests, with two hundreds. He reached the first of these in Adelaide with a six over long-on. Dexter and Cowdrey supported him well, and with the ball Trueman and Titmus took 20 and 21 wickets.

The outstanding bowlers for Australia were the old firm of Davidson and McKenzie, whilst the batting was consistent with nine averaging over 30.

The Duke of Norfolk, Ted Dexter and Alec Bedser at Heathrow en route for Australia

David Sheppard had come back for two Tests against Pakistan after an absence of two years preparing for his priesthood. He was selected for this tour and scored a fine hundred in the second Test at Melbourne, which England deservedly won, only to lose the next at Sydney. Unfortunately, David's two-year absence made him rather rusty in the field. Previously a brilliant close catcher, he dropped quite a few (left) which prompted Freddie Trueman to comment: 'When the Reverend puts his two hands together he should have a better chance than any of us.'

There was also the young English couple who had settled in Australia. When they had a baby the wife said: 'We'll get the Reverend David to christen it.' 'Not likely,' said the husband quickly, 'he'd only drop it!'

At Adelaide he did catch a high ball at long-on, and threw the ball up in the air several times to show his delight. He was interrupted by a shout from the bowler Brian Statham telling him to throw it back at once, as it was a no-ball and the batsmen were still running!

An unusual feature of the tour was that MCC chose a Duke to be their manager – the Duke of Norfolk. He was immensely popular with the Australians who called him 'Dukey'. Wherever MCC played he used to lease a race-horse and run it in the local meeting. He did this at Adelaide and went to the small country race-course of Gawlor to see his horse run. As he walked across the paddock to see his horse, standing under a eucalyptus tree, to his horror he saw the trainer give the horse something to eat. So, thinking it might be a stimulant or drug, he said to the trainer: 'We don't want any funny business. What's that you gave the horse to eat?' 'Oh, only a lump of sugar Your Grace. I'm going to have one myself. Would you like one too?' The trainer ate his lump and to humour him the Duke also ate his, and went off to watch the race from the stewards' stand.

When the little jockey came up to the Duke's horse for his instructions for the race, the trainer said: 'This is a seven furlong race. For the first five furlongs sit quietly and get tucked in behind the others. For the last two furlongs give him all you've got, and if anyone passes you after that it will either be the Duke of Norfolk or myself!'

1963

This was the year when I became the BBC's first cricket correspondent, although continuing to do all Tests for TV. It was a West Indian summer which produced possibly the most exciting and dramatic Test Match I had ever seen — the second Test at Lord's. It had everything: brilliant batting, great fast bowling, five days of excitement and a nail-biting finish. The fortunes of each side changed almost hourly throughout the match.

Even the start was sensational, Conrad Hunte hitting the first three balls for 4. The bowler was Freddie Trueman and it was lucky that the TV viewers were not able to lip-read!

The scoring throughout the match was remarkably even. West Indies 301 and 229, England 297 and 228 for 9. The thrilling climax came at the close of the fifth day when, with one over to be bowled by Wes Hall, England needed 8 runs to win with 2 wickets in hand. But one of these was Colin Cowdrey (right) whose broken left wrist was in plaster, after being struck by a ball from Wes Hall (below). David Allen and Derek Shackleton were the batsmen and they ran singles off the second and third balls. Off the fourth, Shackleton called for a quick single, and Worrell, at short leg, instead of throwing the ball at the stumps at the bowler's end, ran with the ball, raced Shackleton, and whipped off the bails to run him out (opposite page). So Cowdrey had to come in with two balls to go, 6 runs needed for victory. David Allen was the batsman, and resisting the temptation to try to hit a winning six, played out the last two balls safely.

Cowdrey later said that if he had had to bat, he would have turned round and batted left-handed with his good right hand holding the bat. It was a thrilling finish and proved that a drawn game is not necessarily dull.

1963

Outstanding memories of the match:

1. Ted Dexter's 70 in 81 minutes (below, left) *attacked the fast bowling brilliantly with powerful strokes off both front and back foot. It still remains the best innings under a hundred which I have seen in Test cricket.*

2. *The fine sustained fast bowling of* Wes Hall (below, right) *and* Charlie Griffith (opposite, top) *in both innings. But they were rightly criticised for only bowling 14 overs an hour on the last afternoon. It was a fair over-rate by modern standards but was one of the earliest examples of a deliberate ploy to prevent a side from scoring fast enough to win. It undoubtedly cost England the match.*

3. *The tremendous courage of Brian Close who in his fighting second innings of 70 took many balls deliberately on his body, and was battered black and blue* (opposite below), *beyond the call of duty.*

4. I was commentating on TV when the last over was about to start just before 6 pm. Believe it or not, I was told in my ear-phones to hand back to Alexandra Palace for the News. An incredible decision at such a moment. But luckily the boss of BBC TV at the time was Kenneth Adam, a cricket fanatic. He was watching in his office and heard what I had said. The News was just beginning with some item about President Kennedy. Kenneth immediately picked up his 'phone and ordered Alexandra Palace to interrupt the News at once and return to Lord's. This happened and we got the whole of the last over. What a triumph for cricket. I cannot see it happening today, when the News seems to be sacrosanct.

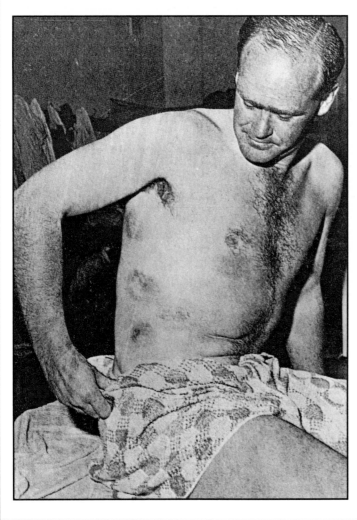

1964

I never thought that I would see Colin Cowdrey hugging Freddie Trueman. But it happened during the third day of the fifth Test at The Oval (below). Australia had made a good reply to England's 182 and with their score at 343 for 6, Ted Dexter seemed at a loss to know whom to put on to bowl. Whilst he was looking indecisive Fred, who up to then had taken no wickets, appeared to take the ball away from Ted and to start immediately measuring out his run. The result was sensational. He got Redpath and McKenzie with successive balls and went into lunch on a hat trick. He didn't get it but eventually moved one away from his old friend Neil Hawke who snicked the ball to Colin Cowdrey at first slip for a catch (opposite). Fred thus became the first Test bowler to take 300 wickets. Cowdrey rushed down the pitch to give Fred his celebrated hug, which featured on the front page of the Sunday papers. It was a great performance by Fred, his 300 wickets coming in only 65 Tests.

Another Yorkshireman will also remember this match: Geoff Boycott scoring the first of his 22 Test hundreds.

There was also a unique happening, at least so far as Test cricket goes. Ted Dexter drove at a ball and his bat split in two, half of it reaching cover point. Luckily for the maker, I don't think we could read the name on the bat on TV.

Australia won a rather mediocre series 1–0, winning by 7 wickets in the third test at Headingley thanks to a fine innings of 160 by Peter Burge.

1964

After that, Bobby Simpson (left) was obviously determined to take no risks in the last two Tests. In the fourth at Old Trafford on a good pitch he went on batting into the third day before declaring at 656 for 8. He himself made 311 in 12¾ hours. Remarkably, it was his first hundred in 34 Tests. I was later to see four other innings of over 300 (John Edrich 310 in 1965 at Headingley, Bob Cowper 307 in 1966 at Melbourne, Lawrence Rowe 302 at Barbados in 1974 and Graham Gooch 333 in 1990 at Lord's). I must admit that it does get a bit monotonous watching the same batsman for ten hours or more.

Most of us thought that England would be pushed to save the follow-on. But Dexter (174) and Barrington (256) (below) put on 246 for the 3rd wicket, and England made 611. Barrington's previous highest score in a Test in England had been 87. It is the only instance in Test cricket of two sides both making over 600 in the same Test.

South Africa

MCC's tour of South Africa was my first visit to that beautiful country. I was especially pleased to go there because my sister had lived in Zululand for nearly 30 years, and so I had the first opportunity of meeting her since then. We had an emotional meeting in Durban where England won the only Test which was not a draw. This was largely due to some subtle spin bowling by Fred Titmus (above seen clean bowling Goddard) and David Allen, and a fine 148 not out by Ken Barrington, who as usual had a highly successful tour, scoring 508 runs at an average of 101.60 in the five Tests.

David Allen bowls Tony Pithey for 85 in the second Test.

Barrington also produced a remarkable piece of bowling in the third Test at Cape Town. When put on to bowl with a draw the only possible result, he decided to liven things up. He did a life-like impersonation of Jim Laker with his slow walk back, that look Jim always gave to heaven as he turned, then the high action, off-spin and all. Net result, his analysis read: 3.1 overs, 1 maiden, 4 runs, 3 wickets! No one was more surprised than he was. Had he been batting he might equally well have given his famous impersonation of W.G. Grace with a large black beard and a fast jerky back stroke as seen on the only film available of W.G.

Sportsman that he was, he also gave himself out caught at the wicket, after the umpire had turned down a confident South African appeal.

Mike Smith had taken over the captaincy from Ted Dexter for this tour. Ted was standing as Conservative candidate against Jim Callaghan in Cardiff, so joined the tour after he had inevitably been defeated. Mike had already proved himself a popular captain with the players, press and opposition on the 1963 tour of India.

Once again, he didn't put a foot wrong. He was friendly, a great debunker of pomposity or conceit, a good tactician and he also set a good example in the field. He never asked anyone to do anything which he wouldn't do himself, and used to crouch perilously near at forward short leg in his glasses. He had a great sense of humour but was a bit cagey when being interviewed (left).

One interesting aspect of the laws cropped up at Durban. In bad light David Brown (right) was sent in as night-watchman. He hadn't got half-way to the pitch when the two umpires called play off for the day. Although he had not received a ball, because he had stepped on to the field of play, he was rightly considered to have started his innings and at the start next morning he had to come in to bat.

1965

Mike Smith continued as captain for the double series against New Zealand and South Africa. England won all three Tests v. New Zealand, but lost 0–1 to South Africa. At Headingley, John Edrich played an amazing innings of 310 not out against New Zealand. He hit five sixes and 52 fours – the highest number of boundaries in any Test innings. Of all opening batsmen whom I have seen I consider him to have been the best judge of line on or outside his off stump. He often left balls alone on purpose which were only missing his stumps by inches.

My old friend Ken Barrington slightly blotted his copy-book at Edgbaston, when he made 137 in the first Test against New Zealand. He got stuck on 85 for 62 minutes (20 overs were bowled). He then crept slowly to his hundred in singles, but as soon as he had reached it he immediately hit Pollard for 14 in one over, including a big drive for 6. Not surprisingly he was slated by the press for appearing to care more about his hundred than for the needs of his team. He was dropped for the next Test and I drove him back to London. He was in a miserable state of mind and couldn't explain why he had done it.

After missing the Lord's Test he was selected for Headingley where he made 163!

The series against South Africa was Pollock time, Peter the elder brother (below, left) and fast bowler taking 20 wickets in the three Tests, and 21-year-old Graeme (below, right) making most runs (291) including a

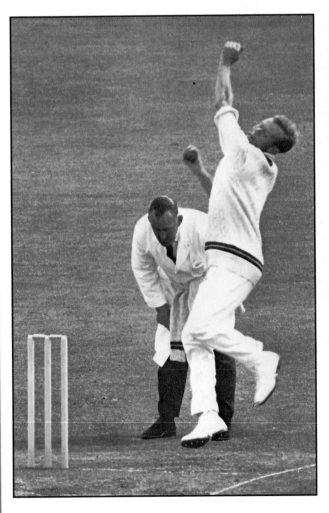

truly great innings at Trent Bridge. In damp, difficult conditions he made 125 in only 140 minutes, the last 91 coming in 70 minutes. I shall never forget the power of his off-drives through extra cover, and his forcing strokes off the back foot, all round the wicket. It was superlative and I have always reckoned him in my top eight batsmen.

One other feature of the South African side was their brilliant athletic fielding with Colin Bland (left) in the covers as the star. He could come in at full speed, pick the ball up on the run, and in one movement throw down the stumps with unnerving accuracy. He could knock down a single stump from quite a distance, a skill he achieved by practising for hours throwing at a stump in a hockey net. We were televising their match against Kent at Canterbury and persuaded Colin to give a demonstration during the tea interval. He put up three stumps and knocked them down one after the other before an admiring crowd of incredulous schoolboys. What an example for them to follow.

Incidentally, in this match Graeme Pollock scored a magnificent 203 not out. This enabled the older members in the crowd to compare with their own idol Frank Woolley. I was lucky to have seen them both. They each enjoyed hitting the ball hard and especially liked to hit sixes. (Graeme had five in this innings.) Whereas Pollock seemed to score through the power of his strokes, Woolley appeared more graceful and to rely more on his timing. But give me either of them for a perfect day's cricket.

<u>Australia</u>

Another enjoyable tour under Mike Smith's captaincy, the highlight for England being the third Test at Sydney which they won by an innings. Bob Barber (left) put on 234 for the 1st wicket with Geoff Boycott, and played a superbly aggressive innings of 185 watched by his father Jack standing on the Hill. In Australia's first innings David Brown bowled fast and accurately for 5 for 63, and when Australia followed on, Fred Titmus and David Allen spun them out on a wearing pitch, taking 4 wickets apiece.

Australia retaliated by winning the fourth Test at Adelaide by an innings. The other three Tests were all drawn. In the first at Brisbane there was a dramatic start when Bill Lawry (below) survived a confident appeal for a catch by Jim Parks behind

the wicket before he had scored. He went on to make 166 in 7 hours, and England felt a bit sore as they were certain that he had hit it. But Bill was not a 'walker' and believed that it was up to the umpire to judge.

We also saw the arrival in Test cricket of a magnificent 19-year-old stroke player, Doug Walters (right). He scored 155, being particularly severe on the spinners. His footwork was always a delight to watch, but against fast bowlers he was vulnerable outside the off stump and Mike Smith normally set two gullies for him. He was a chain-smoker, and kept puffing away right up to the time he had to go in to bat.

Ken Barrington (below) had his inevitably successful tour, and finished with a century in each of the last two Tests. For years he was England's sheet anchor, usually concentrating on defence. But in the fifth Test at Melbourne he played one of the fastest ever Test hundreds, reaching it in under two and a half hours, and completing it once again with a six over long-on − an especially big hit on the vast Melbourne ground.

After that, we had to endure Bob Cowper accumulating 307 runs. I have known better entertainment.

1966

The West Indies under Gary Sobers were welcome visitors and won the series 3–1. Mike Smith lost the captaincy after England's defeat at Old Trafford. Colin Cowdrey was captain in the next three, two of which were lost. At The Oval Brian Close took over and his aggressive captaincy paid off, England winning by an innings.

The Lord's Test saw the dramatic return of 39-year-old Tom Graveney (below), after an absence of three years from Test cricket. He delighted the crowd with a typically graceful 96. In complete contrast, Colin Milburn gave a devastating display of power, making 126 not out. This followed his 94 in his first Test at Old Trafford, after being run out for 0 in the first innings. He brought an air of gaiety into Test cricket and with his Billy Bunter figure was immensely popular with the crowds. Lord's was also Basil D'Oliveira's first Test for England.

For West Indies at Lord's there was a match saving stand of 274 by Gary Sobers and his cousin David Holford (both seen opposite – Sobers with bat). In fact, Gary had a wonderful tour making 722 runs with three hundreds and 94 and 81, plus taking 20 wickets and holding ten catches. Undoubtedly the greatest ever all-rounder – begging W.G.'s pardon!

At The Oval Graveney again shone with 165 (run out), and J.T. Murray matched him for style and elegance with 112. But the outstanding performance came from England's No. 10 and No. 11, Ken Higgs and John Snow (both seen right – Higgs nearest the camera). They put on 128 for the last wicket in only 140 minutes. It was just two runs short of Wilfred Rhodes's and R.E. Foster's record last wicket stand for England. The amazing fact about this tenth wicket stand was that it contained both Higgs's and Snow's maiden fifties in first-class cricket. Thanks largely to them England, after being 166 for 7, finished with 527.

1967

Not a very memorable year with a terribly wet May – the wettest for two hundred years, and a double tour with India and Pakistan. India lost all their Tests and Pakistan two of theirs, drawing the first at Lord's thanks to 187 not out by Hanif Mohammad (below) the 'Little Master'. It took him nine hours, and strangely was the only Test hundred he ever made in three tours of England. (He made eleven others.)

In contrast at The Oval Asif Iqbal, a fine stroke player, made a brilliant 146 and with Intikhab put on 190 for the 9th wicket. This is still the record for all Test cricket. A feature of any innings by Asif was his fast running between the wickets. I would place him, Mike Griffith, Tony Pawson and Clive Radley as the quickest I have seen between the wickets.

India, under the Nawab of Pataudi, was handicapped by the weather and a string of injuries, and was easily beaten in all three Tests, in spite of a second innings of 510 in a great fight back at Headingley. Pataudi himself made 64 and 148 in this match – not bad with only one eye.

For England, Boycott (left) made 246 not out, his highest Test score. But it took him nine and a half hours and he was dropped from the next Test as a disciplinary measure. Unusually for him he actually hit a six!

In spite of captaining England to five victories, the season finished tragically for Brian Close. Just before the last Test, Yorkshire played Warwickshire at Edgbaston. Warwickshire were set 142 to win in 100 minutes and when they looked like winning, Close resorted to time-wasting tactics.

In the last fifteen minutes Yorkshire only bowled two overs, and at one time went off for rain leaving the batsmen and two umpires still on the pitch.

As luck would have it the selectors were meeting at Lord's to select the MCC captain for the forthcoming tour of the West Indies. On his form during the summer Close was a certainty. But he was summoned to Lord's (right, with Dick Gabey, Club Superintendent of the MCC) and asked to give a guarantee that he would never employ such tactics in the West Indies. He is a true Yorkshireman, obstinate and honest, and he felt he could not give that guarantee. So Colin Cowdrey was elected in his place.

Ironically, since he had been selected for all six Tests, Close went straight down to The Oval and led England to victory with Colin Cowdrey playing under him.

The whole affair was tragic and unnecessary and it changed the whole of Close's future.

1967—68

<u>West Indies</u>

The tour to West Indies was Colin Cowdrey's first as MCC captain, though he had been vice-captain four times before. Thanks largely to the way he ran the tour it was a very happy one, capped by England winning the series 1—0. They won the fourth Test at Port of Spain thanks to a 'gentlemanly' declaration by Gary Sobers which made him the most unpopular man in the West Indies for a short time. England would also have won the first Test but for an unlikely but defiant 26 not out by Wes Hall, of all people.

But my outstanding memory of the tour was the dramatic drawn fifth Test at Georgetown. It matched the 1963 drawn match at Lord's for a thrilling climax.

Gary answered his critics with two superb innings of 152 and 95 not out. John Snow bowled at his fastest and best to take 10 wickets in the match on a slowish pitch more suitable to spinners and took 27 wickets in the series.

In reply to the West Indies' 414 England were struggling at 259 for 8 until Tony Lock, who had just been flown from Australia as a replacement for Fred Titmus, put on 109 for the 9th wicket with Pat Pocock. Lock hit out at all the bowlers, and his 89 was his highest score in first-class cricket. In contrast, Pat defended stubbornly, batting for 82 minutes before making his first run.

The climax came on the last day when England, set 308 to win, were quite happy just to play for a draw and so win the series. So much for good intentions. Thanks to some masterly spin bowling by Lance Gibbs after an hour and a half they were 41 for 5. In spite of the pitch helping the spin of Gibbs and Sobers, Cowdrey and Knott had a stand of 127. Cowdrey was then out for 82, but Knott stayed for four hours to finish with 73 not out, improvising as only he could. He defended most of the time but when the loose ball came along he hit it for 4, and actually hit 14 fours — a very high percentage. He gradually ran out of partners and when Pocock was given out caught off what looked like a bump ball, Jeff Jones was left to play out the last over from Lance Gibbs. Jeff was a good fast left-arm bowler but a true No. 11 bat. However, somehow he survived, playing every ball with his pads — some deliberately, others not.

So England at 206 for 9 drew the match and won the series. But it had been a far too close run thing for the good of my nerves.

There were two events which temporarily marred the tour.

1. In the second Test at Kingston in West Indies' second innings, Basil Butcher was given out, caught by Parks from a diving leg-side catch off D'Oliveira. The West Indies were in trouble at the time. After following on they were then 204 for 5 and the crowd did not like it. They started throwing bottles on to the field and, in spite of a brave appeal to them to stop by Colin Cowdrey, they continued to bombard the field. The police then decided to use tear gas but misjudged the direction of the wind. As a result the tear gas was blown away from the crowd, passed the press box and went across the ground to the pavilion (opposite page). In the press box people were crying and we had to stop broadcasting because we couldn't speak. In the pavilion, the VIPs took refuge in the loos and chaos temporarily reigned. England, upset by the riot, instead of

winning the game as had seemed likely, nearly lost it during 85 extra minutes which were allotted on an extra day.

2. The other event was a bathing accident involving Fred Titmus when we were relaxing on the St James's beach in Barbados (see over). He went into the sea to push out a small boat which, unknown to him, had a propeller underneath instead of at the stern. His legs were sucked under and four toes on his left foot were cut off, but luckily not his big toe on which one depends for balance. Amazingly, he felt no pain except that he thought he had been stung by a jelly-fish. Luckily for him the toes were only cut about three quarters of the way down so that it didn't affect the nerves where the toe joins the foot. They were stitched up very efficiently and he was flown home. Remarkably, three months later he was playing again for Middlesex wearing a special boot. Even more remarkable was that he took 111 wickets and made 924 runs during the season.

Incidentally, the pitch at Kingston had more and bigger cracks in its surface than I or any of the players had ever seen. It was like a giant mosaic puzzle, but surprisingly played quite well.

One other interesting side to the tour was that BBC TV sent out a film unit, and Denis Compton and I did the commentary. At the end of each day the film was flown back to London. It was unusual because with only one camera and no monitor to watch it was difficult for us to know exactly what the cameraman was filming, and he had to try to follow whatever we were talking about. It sounds and was complicated, but somehow it worked.

Another wet summer spoilt the series against the Australians. Under Bill Lawry, they were a weak bowling side and lacked real class in their batting. But they did win the first Test, lost the fifth and drew the series to keep the Ashes.

The Edgbaston Test was a personal triumph for England's captain Colin Cowdrey (below). It was his hundredth Test, he made his twenty-first Test hundred, and when he reached 60 joined Wally Hammond as the only other person at that time to make 7000 runs in Test cricket.

A triumph of a different sort awaited him at The Oval where England had to win to draw the series.

Thanks to John Edrich (164) and Basil D'Oliveira (158) England made 494. Dolly was a late selection when Roger Prideaux had to withdraw through illness. The Chairman of selectors, Doug Insole, rang Colin Cowdrey about a replacement batsman. But Colin suddenly decided he wanted an extra bowler who could also bat, and asked for Dolly. By that decision the history of cricket was changed.

1968

Dolly (left) was lucky to be missed by Barry Jarman when 31, but his fine innings and steady bowling made him everyone's selection for the winter tour of South Africa — except the selectors. But more of that later.

Australia had to get 352 to win at The Oval and at lunch on the last day were in serious trouble at 86 for 5, and all odds were on an easy England victory. It had been a glorious sunny morning but when they came off for lunch dark clouds suddenly appeared and within minutes there was a tremendous storm which turned the whole ground into a lot of miniature lakes (below). The storm stopped as quickly as it had started and the sun came out, but further play looked impossible.

However the ground began to dry quickly under the hot sun, and the lakes began to disappear. An impatient Cowdrey refused to give up, and over the loud speaker an appeal was made for volunteers from the crowd to help with the mopping up operations. It was a unique sight, fifty or so volunteers armed with brooms and blankets. They were so successful that the umpires decided that play should restart at 4.45 pm leaving 75 minutes for play, and for England to try to take 5 wickets.

Inverarity and Jarman defended bravely for 35 minutes, and Cowdrey put on D'Oliveira to bowl. The move paid off, Dolly getting Jarman in his second over. Then came a dramatic collapse as Dolly was immediately replaced by Derek Underwood who proceeded to take the last 4 wickets for 6 runs, and England won with five minutes to spare. It was a thrilling finish and hats off to the Australian batsmen for not wasting time. But England's biggest debt was to the army of mopper-uppers who had made play possible.

I still think that the photograph of Underwood trapping Inverarity lbw (below) is one of the best ever cricket pictures. Everyone in the England team is in the picture as they surround the batsman, and turn round as one man to appeal to umpire Charlie Elliott.

1968

On the Wednesday and Thursday after the Oval Test the selectors met at Lord's to choose the MCC team to go to South Africa that winter. There was enormous interest in the media who all pressed for D'Oliveira's inclusion although they knew that it might prejudice the tour. Just before 6 pm on the Thursday I was waiting with a microphone outside the door of the committee room, so that I could be the first to announce the team on the Six O'clock News. There was tension everywhere as MCC secretary Billy Griffith came out and gave me a list of the team. I quickly divided it up into batsmen, bowlers, wicket-keepers and all-rounders, which was the way I always gave out the teams over the air. In a few minutes the News called me up and I read out the list, and suddenly realised that what people were really waiting for was the names of the all-rounders at the end. Would one of them be Dolly? The first I read out was Ken Barrington, whom I always regarded as an all-rounder. He told me afterwards that as he wasn't among the batsmen he thought he had not been selected. Then came the crunch with the last name – it was Tom Cartwright not Dolly. The rest is history. A few days later, Cartwright had to withdraw through injury, and the selectors promptly chose Dolly as a replacement, although unwisely they had publicly said that they regarded Dolly only as a batsman overseas.

12 *The Daily Telegraph, Thursday, August 29, 1968*

MCC IGNORE D'OLIVEIRA AND MILBURN

TEAM FOR SOUTH AFRICA LACKS THIRD SPINNER

By E. W. SWANTON

M.C.C. have announced their team of 16 for South Africa save for a vacant place left in hopes of Jeffrey Jones, of Glamorgan, becoming fully fit before the party leaves in early November. Basil d'Oliveira is not included.

I think the omission of d'Oliveira substantially weakens the strength and balance of the side, but before commenting on that let me regard it as it stands.

With an average age of 29 it is old by modern standards. It is also overloaded with specialists. In d'Oliveira's absence its only all-rounder is Barrington.

That is a title which may occasion this hardened warrior some amusement, but there is little doubt that at the age of 37 he must thank his considerable, if under-used, skill as a wrist-spinner for the opportunity of making his ninth tour with M C C.

There are two omissions specially to be regretted in addition to that of d'Oliveira: That of Milburn — has Lord's '68 been so quickly forgotten? — and of a third regular spin bowler, be he Wilson, or Gifford, or Birkenshaw, or Hobbs, or — well, almost anyone.

The party

	Age
M. C. Cowdrey (Kent, capt.)	35
T. W. Graveney (Worcs, vice-cap.)	41
K. F. Barrington (Surrey)	37
G. Boycott (Yorkshire)	27
D. J. Brown (Warwickshire)	26
T. W. Cartwright (Warwickshire)	33
R. M. H. Cottam (Hampshire)	23
J. H. Edrich (Surrey)	31
K. W. R. Fletcher (Essex)	24
A. P. Knott (Kent)	22
J. T. Murray (Middlesex)	33
R. M. Prideaux (Northamptonshire)	29
P. I. Pocock (Surrey)	21
J. A. Snow (Sussex)	26
D. L. Underwood (Kent)	23

One other fast bowler to be selected.

The South African Prime Minister, Mr Vorster, then announced that he could not receive a team forced on South Africa by 'political' influence, and MCC accordingly cancelled the tour forthwith.

Luckily, MCC were able to arrange instead a short tour of Sri Lanka and Pakistan. But talk about political influence!

Pakistan

I covered the three Tests in Pakistan and they were all spoilt by political or student demonstrations. The police seemed powerless. Les Ames did a great job as Colin Cowdrey's manager. He would have called off the tour after the interrupted first Test at Lahore, had he not been implored to carry on by the British High Commission. In fact, for the second Test in Dacca, Les made a pact with the students who promised to control the crowds themselves if MCC would play, provided though that there would not be a single policeman on the ground. There wasn't, and it worked!

The Third Test at Karachi coincided with a general strike and the locals were also incensed that their hero Hanif had not been appointed captain. England batted for two and a third days and had made 502–7 by just before lunch on the third day. Alan Knott – 96 not out – was approaching his maiden Test hundred, and with his partner David Brown had put on 75 for the 8th wicket. Suddenly, the students in the crowd erupted and made a beeline for the players, swarming across the ground. Knott and Brown, in spite of their pads, must have broken the 75 yards world record as they sprinted to the pavilion. They just made it before the rioters started to burn down the stands.

I was doing TV for Pakistan at the time and was describing the scenes, when the Pakistan TV authorities pulled the plug out, and I too was able to sprint round to the back of the pavilion. We were all shut up there for about an hour and and left the ground under escort. Not surprisingly the match – and the tour – was immediately abandoned, and by a miracle of organisation, Les Ames arranged for us all to fly back to England that night.

But to go back to the cricket for a moment. The England innings contained two hundreds by Tom Graveney and Colin Milburn (right), who made a brilliant 139, reaching his century off only 163 balls.

1968–69

It was sadly to be his last Test innings. He had been flown in at short notice from Perth in Australia to replace Colin Cowdrey, who had had to go home as his father-in-law had died.

When Ollie arrived at Dacca the MCC team were very down in the dumps, and fed up with all the goings-on. But he cheered everyone up as we all welcomed him at the airport where, garlanded with flowers, he stood on the steps of the aircraft and sang his theme song, 'The Green, Green Grass of Home'. He had been too tired to play at Dacca but made amends at Karachi.

He and I used to sing 'Underneath the Arches' and 'Me and My Shadow' together. We were pleasantly surprised that after one party where we had performed, Saeed Ahmed, the Pakistan captain (left), presented us with two expensive looking presents!

There was a double tour by West Indies and New Zealand, England beating them both 2–0. There was little outstanding to recall about the six Tests, England owing much of her success to good bowling by John Snow, David Brown and Derek Underwood, plus two typical hundreds by John Edrich.

But one or two dates stick in my memory.

Sunday, 27th April. The start of the John Player's County League on Sundays, which in 1987 became the Refuge Assurance League.

These 40-overs-a-side games have brought much welcome finance to the counties, and attracted a new type of spectator – the families, most welcome, the drinking louts far less so. But sadly it has seriously affected the technique of many first-class cricketers. Cross-batted strokes, the 'steer' through the slips, defensive bowling to contain rather than take wickets, defensive field placing and, until recently, the scorning of spin bowlers. But there are signs now that the spinners are being used more and what's more are taking wickets. But some are still told to bowl flat by their captains. A welcome exception to all these minuses is the fielding and throwing, which have improved to the highest possible standard, and are now an entertainment in themselves.

Saturday, 24th May. I was commentating at the annual Whitsun match between Middlesex and Sussex at Lord's. At about 12.30 pm I was rung up by the BBC News and asked to do a piece about Colin Milburn (below) into the One O'clock News. They told me that he had had a car accident on Friday night and had lost the sight of his left eye. It happened just after Northants had beaten the West Indies. It was shattering news, not just to the world of cricket, but to me personally. Cricket was his life and he had no other interest except the companionship of his cricketer colleagues over a glass (or two!) of beer. He brought fun and excitement on to the field, and laughter and universal friendship off it. Following his 139 v. Pakistan he had started the season with a brilliant century against Leicestershire. He scored 158 in only 77 overs with five sixes and 16 fours. What a loss he was to cricket, though at the BBC we were glad to welcome him to the commentary box both on TV and the radio. He talked much good sense mixed with cheerful chatter. He was a loveable, very human man and his countless friends mourned his sudden death in 1990.

1969

Sunday, 25th May. *Another accident to an England player brought a change in the England captaincy. Colin Cowdrey, batting for Kent in a John Player match at Maidstone, tore his achilles tendon. I was on the ground and I promise you I heard the snap as it went. This put him out of action for the season. It meant that just as he had established himself as England's captain he would have to forego his life's ambition to captain England against Australia in Australia. He was replaced by Ray Illingworth who then started his long reign of 31 Tests as England's captain. Rotten luck for Colin but at least he went as vice-captain under Illingworth, believe it or not, for the fifth time.*

Thursday, 24th July. *I shall never forget one of my worst gaffes. Alan Ward (below), in his first Test, was bowling very fast from the pavilion end at Lord's to Geoff Turner of New Zealand. Off the fifth ball of his over he hit Turner a nasty blow in the box. Geoff collapsed in the crease and the cameras panned in to show him writhing in pain. As he lay there I waffled away pretending he had been hit anywhere except where he had been, as it was a bit rude. After a couple of minutes he staggered to his feet and someone handed him his bat. I said: 'He looks a bit pale and shaken but he's pluckily going to continue batting. One ball left!'*

There was no MCC tour scheduled for 1969–70, so I was surprised and delighted to receive an unusual invitation from Charles Fortune in South Africa to be the 'neutral' commentator with Alan McGilvray and himself (both photographed with me, right) in the four-Test series against Australia. We were to do 15 minutes each with no summariser between overs. It was an experiment, and although so far as I know it has never been repeated anywhere, the South Africans evidently liked it.

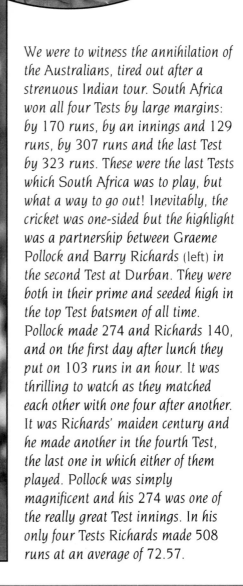

We were to witness the annihilation of the Australians, tired out after a strenuous Indian tour. South Africa won all four Tests by large margins: by 170 runs, by an innings and 129 runs, by 307 runs and the last Test by 323 runs. These were the last Tests which South Africa was to play, but what a way to go out! Inevitably, the cricket was one-sided but the highlight was a partnership between Graeme Pollock and Barry Richards (left) in the second Test at Durban. They were both in their prime and seeded high in the top Test batsmen of all time. Pollock made 274 and Richards 140, and on the first day after lunch they put on 103 runs in an hour. It was thrilling to watch as they matched each other with one four after another. It was Richards' maiden century and he made another in the fourth Test, the last one in which either of them played. Pollock was simply magnificent and his 274 was one of the really great Test innings. In his only four Tests Richards made 508 runs at an average of 72.57.

What a waste of players, and what a loss to spectators everywhere, when both of them were cut off from Test cricket by politics when in their prime.

During the tour I had many opportunities to talk to the South African captain Ali Backer and his vice-captain Eddie Barlow about their forthcoming tour to England in the summer. There was much speculation. Would it or would it not take place? There were already threats of violence and disruption from anti-South African groups in England, stirred up by Peter Hain. John Woodcock, Michael Melford and I used to rehearse Backer and Barlow in TV technique, in preparation for the hostile interviews they would undoubtedly be faced with in England. I assumed the role of Robin Day and put the toughest questions I could think of. It was good fun but also a useful exercise.

I was prepared for a cricket crisis when I returned to England in mid-March. But I was not expecting an unwelcome piece of personal news. The first person I met at the BBC was Neil Durden-Smith who welcomed me back and said: 'I am sorry you are not going to do TV commentary this summer.' This was news to me, and I suppose in a novel I would have clutched my heart and turned deathly pale. It was rather a shock since I had been doing TV since it restarted in 1946, and no one had said anything about my being dropped after 24 years. So I hurried off to see my boss, the Head of Outside Broadcasts, Robert Hudson. 'Oh yes,' he said, 'haven't they told you?' He went on to say that he was sorry for me but in another way delighted because he wanted me to become one of the Test Match Special team on radio. As you can imagine this kind gesture was a terrific relief for me and started my 20 years of happiness on Radio 3's Test Match Special. Oh, and by the way, I still *haven't* heard from BBC TV nor did I receive a word of thanks from them for having helped develop TV commentary during the first 24 post-war years. I think that at least they could have uttered one of Arthur Askey's favourite catch-phrases: 'Ta ever so'.

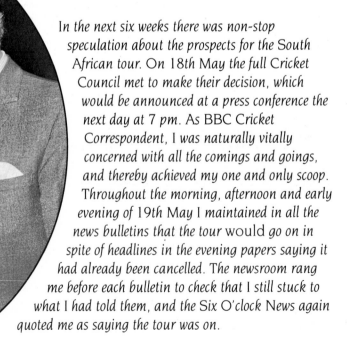

In the next six weeks there was non-stop speculation about the prospects for the South African tour. On 18th May the full Cricket Council met to make their decision, which would be announced at a press conference the next day at 7 pm. As BBC Cricket Correspondent, I was naturally vitally concerned with all the comings and goings, and thereby achieved my one and only scoop. Throughout the morning, afternoon and early evening of 19th May I maintained in all the news bulletins that the tour would *go on in spite* of headlines in the evening papers saying it had already been cancelled. The newsroom rang me before each bulletin to check that I still stuck to what I had told them, and the Six O'clock News again quoted me as saying the tour was on.

At 7pm at Lord's in a crowded press conference Billy Griffith (seen opposite on the left with Maurice Allom), after a short preamble, announced in a deathly hush: 'The Council have decided by a substantial majority that the tour should proceed as arranged.' The press was stunned and rushed off to 'phone their papers. But my lone stand had been vindicated and I couldn't resist giving a wink to my Mole. Yes, I did have a Mole, that's how scoops are made. I hadn't asked him for direct information when I rang him early on 19th May. All I said was: 'How many marks out of ten would you give me if I said the tour was going to go on?' 'Oh,' he replied after a short pause, 'about nine and a half'. That was good enough for me.

Of course, it was all short-lived. On 21st May the Home Secretary, Jim Callaghan, invited Maurice Allom, Chairman of the Cricket Council, and its Secretary, Billy Griffith, to meet him at the Home Office. The next day the government cancelled the tour. A few weeks later, on 17th June, it was defeated in the General Election. I wonder if there was any connection?

The TCCB which together with the Cricket Council had only been set up since 1968, quickly arranged a series of five Test Matches between England and a very strong Rest of the World side. At the time, the BBC was assured that the matches would be given full Test status. Wisden the following year called them Test Matches and included their scores in the Test records. But later all this was changed. They were no longer classified as Tests by the cricket authorities, and all their records were kept separate from Test records.

With such a mixture of great players assembled in one team, there was some splendid and entertaining cricket. It was an ideal introduction for me on Test Match Special. The Rest of the World won 4, and England 1. But the results did not really matter. Cricket had fought back against its enemies and provided a perfect summer's cricket. The Rest of the World captain, Gary Sobers, and Clive Lloyd (above) each made two hundreds, and surprisingly Ray Illingworth scored most runs for England with an average of 52.88. John Snow was the pick of the England bowlers, and Sobers and Barlow for the Rest of the World.

Australia

Ray Illingworth captained the MCC team to Australia and by winning the series 2–0 regained the Ashes for England after 12 years. It was my last tour as BBC Cricket Correspondent and there were many moments to savour.

First and foremost was the last ball bowled in the seventh Test at Sydney. (The third Test at Melbourne had been abandoned and an extra Test added in its place.) I was commentating at the time on ABC and back to England on Radio 2, who stayed open all night to get the end of the match. Keith Fletcher caught Jenner off bat and pad at silly point off the bowling of Derek Underwood, and the Ashes were safely ours. Ray Illingworth was 'chaired' off by his team (left) and in celebration I composed the words for the Ashes song to an old music hall tune, 'Show Me Your Winkle Tonight'. The team (seen below rehearsing) recorded it when they got home, but in spite of the kind help of Decca, and Vic Lewis who got together a top class band, the record sadly never reached the Top 10,000!

Features of the tour were Illingworth's captaincy; the batting of Geoff Boycott (657 runs av. 93.85) and John Edrich (648 runs av. 72.00); and the bowling of John Snow (31 wickets).

One unhappy incident marred the final Test when
Ray Illingworth (rightly, in my opinion) led his
team off the field when Snow (right) had been pelted
with bottles and cans, after hitting Jenner with a
bouncer (above). I was glad that two Australian ex-
captains supported my opinion at the time. I was on
the air and saw the whole thing, and had
Illingworth stayed on the field things might have got
worse – as they did on previous tours of the West
Indies when in similar circumstances players stayed
on the field. As it was, everything was soon cleared
up, and play restarted in about a quarter of an
hour.

I made my first visit to New Zealand where
England won the first Test thanks to Derek
Underwood taking 6 for 12 and 6 for 85 on a
damp pitch where the ball kept low. In this match,
Alan Knott kindly stood down so that his loyal
understudy Bob Taylor could play in his first
Test. As a reward from the gods for his kindness,
Knotty made 101 and 96 in the second Test at
Auckland, which was drawn.

1971

A nother double tour shared by Pakistan and India. England beat Pakistan 1–0, but was beaten 0–1 by India – India's first ever victory in England.

In the first Test at Edgbaston, which was drawn, Pakistan made 608–7 dec. with hundreds from Zaheer Abbas (opposite), Mushtaq and Asif. Zaheer, in fact, made a superb 274 with 38 fours, many of them powerful strokes off the back foot, especially on the leg-side. With his spectacles and high back lift he was an outstanding batsman.

The drawn second Test at Lord's was the wettest there since the first Pakistan tour of 1954. England just managed to win at The Oval by 25 runs, Boycott making his third hundred in succession.

After two drawn Tests, India's win at The Oval was an historic occasion for them. It was the first Test they had ever won in England and there was much dancing in the streets and many celebrations back home in India. The Indian Prime Minister even had her plane diverted, so that she could welcome the players home at the airport. I shall always look back on their tour with pleasure because of the joy of seeing three top-class spinners all bowling together in one team. Bedi (left) with his slow, accurate and flighty left arm was a cheerful character in his colourful patka. When the wicket-keeper missed a ball off Bedi, we used to call them 'Bedi Byes'.

1971

Venkat bowled a somewhat flat off-spin, and the jewel in the crown was Chandrasekhar (below) with his medium fast leg-breaks and vicious googlies. He spun India to victory at The Oval with 6 for 38 in England's second innings. He got bounce as well as spin, all the more remarkable because his right arm had been affected by polio. He was said to hum film music as he ran up to bowl.

One unusual feature of the England batting was that John Jameson, now the cricket secretary at MCC, went in first four times and was run out in three of his innings. And Boycott wasn't even playing!

Australia

That winter there was no MCC tour and I was lucky once again to be selected as a 'neutral' commentator, this time by the ABC in Australia. Alan McGilvray, Lindsay Hassett and I covered three of the five matches of a World XI against Australia. These replaced a planned tour by South Africa, and the World XI won 2–1. But once again the results mattered less than some of the fine cricket played, especially by Greg Chappell who averaged 106.25, and Dennis Lillee who took 24 wickets. On the fast Perth pitch he took 8 for 29 in only seven overs, the last 6 wickets for no runs.

For the World XI it was good to see another Graeme Pollock hundred at Adelaide, and Tony Greig's all-round form was a portent for the future. But the most outstanding feat of the whole tour was Gary Sobers's 254 at Melbourne (right), described by Sir Donald Bradman as 'probably the best ever seen in Australia'. I certainly have never seen the like before or since. His scorching drives, hooks and cuts were unforgettable. They left the fielders standing, and by the end even they were applauding his brilliant stroke-play, much of it improvised and unorthodox. He was batting for six and a quarter hours and hit two sixes and 35 fours.

1972

This was my last season as a member of the BBC staff and so I ceased at the end of it to be the Cricket Correspondent. I have been a free-lance ever since. The series against Australia was closely fought between two well-matched sides. It was halved 2–2, so England retained the Ashes.

There was no high scoring for England, the top average being Tony Greig's 36.00. Openers Edrich and Boycott only averaged 21.80 and 18.00 apiece. John Snow continued his fine form with 24 wickets but was overshone by Dennis Lillee (left) with 31. But the man who hit the headlines was Bob Massie (opposite), who in the second Test at Lord's took 8 wickets in each innings in what was his first Test match (8 for 84 and 8 for 53). Only Jim Laker (19) and Sydney Barnes (17) have taken more in one Test. I had seen Bob take 7 wickets in Sydney against the World XI, and it was obvious then that he had the ability to swing the ball away from the batsmen; all his wickets there coming from catches by the slips or wicket-keeper.

At Lord's he had dream conditions with a damp, humid atmosphere and he swung the ball prodigiously and late. It was fascinating to watch him as he ran in round the wicket from the nursery end towards us in the commentary box. Mixed with his outswinger was the occasional late inswinger. In fact 5 of his wickets in the first innings were either bowled or lbw. In the second innings, however, all 8 came from catches, 3 to Greg Chappell at first slip and two to Rodney Marsh behind the wicket.

It was a sensational start to a Test career. But as suddenly as he had arrived, so his ability to swing the ball rapidly declined. He did take 5 more wickets in the third Test but none in the fourth and 2 for 146 in the fifth. Alan Knott by then had worked out how to play him and by standing square on made 92 and 63.

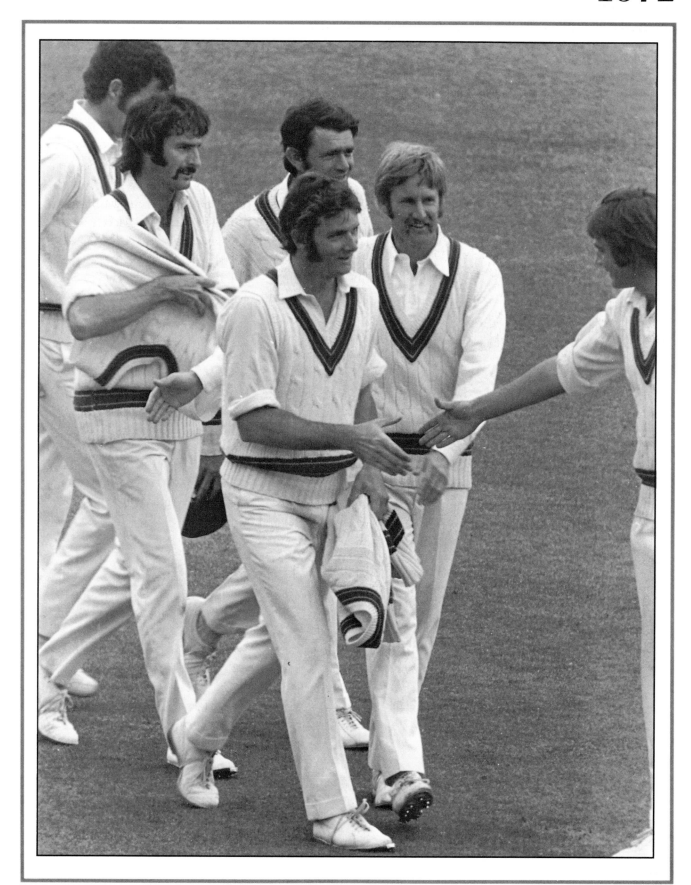

Two other feats are worth mentioning. At Headingley, once again Derek Underwood (opposite) *found a pitch which took spin, and inevitably in those conditions proved too good for the batsmen. He took 10 wickets in the match with his usual immaculate length and medium pace spin.*

At The Oval there was a first-time record. Ian and Greg Chappell put on 201 for the 3rd wicket, both of them *making hundreds, the first time that two brothers had made hundreds in the same innings of a Test* (below, Greg Chappell acknowledges the applause on completing his century).

Finally, 1972 saw the first of the one-day internationals. Sponsored by Prudential, now by Texaco, they have *been a feature of every tour ever since, each visiting team playing two on a double tour but three if playing five Tests.*

I had a field-day for nicknames with this Australian side, with Lillee (Laguna), Massie (Chusetts) and Colley (Melon).

1973

This was a double tour with New Zealand the first visitors. England won 2–0 but this was an unfair reflection of the strength of the two sides.

In the first Test at Trent Bridge, New Zealand, set 479 runs to win, nearly achieved this seemingly impossible task. Thanks to a fighting innings of 176 by their captain Bev Congdon they made 440, just 39 runs short of their target. They had collapsed for only 97 in their first innings in reply to England's 250. But then a couple of hundreds by Dennis Amiss and Tony Greig meant they were set this mammoth target. England owed much to their seam attack of John Snow, Geoff Arnold and Tony Greig. A young tearaway fast bowler aged 21 played only in this Test and his figures were 45–8–143–1. New Zealand journalist Dick Brittenden wrote about him: 'He has considerable prospects of success in the years ahead.' His name was Richard Hadlee (left).

At Lord's, New Zealand replied to England's 253 with another big innings of 551 for 9 dec. There were centuries for Mark Burgess and Vic Pollard. Bev Congdon (seen opposite with Glenn Turner) did not do so well here; he made one less than at Trent Bridge – 175! England only avoided defeat because of a fine 178 by Keith Fletcher who monopolised the bowling to take England to safety. By the close, they had the respectable total of 463 for 9, and so drew the match.

At Trent Bridge there was a case of the 'biter' bit. Geoff Boycott was actually run out himself for a second run which Dennis Amiss refused. Both batsmen ended up at the same end, but Amiss determinedly stayed in his crease, so Boycott was the one out.

The third Test at Headingley was a disappointment to the New Zealanders. On a green pitch they found the same trio of Snow, Arnold and Old too good for them in the conditions, and were easily beaten by an innings and 1 run.

New Zealand would have done far better if its star batsman Glenn Turner had succeeded in the Tests, in which he only averaged 23.20. Perhaps he was too tired out after reaching 1000 runs, with four hundreds, before the end of May.

1973

The second visitors were the West Indies, who won 2–0. Their bowling relied a lot on Keith Boyce who took 19 wickets, but their batting was very strong. Six batsmen averaged over 42, with Sobers (below, left) in terrific form with an average of 76.50, closely followed by Clive Lloyd and Roy Fredericks. In complete contrast, England made under 260 four times, only once topping 300, although Fletcher, Boycott and Amiss all averaged over 46.

I have four special memories of the tour:

1. In the first Test at The Oval it looked as if England had discovered a new quality Test batsman when Frank Hayes (below, right) – in his first Test – made 106 not out. He played the spin of Lance Gibbs and Gary Sobers particularly well. Sadly, he never lived up to this early promise.

2. There was an unpleasant incident in the second Test at Edgbaston. Arthur Fagg turned down a

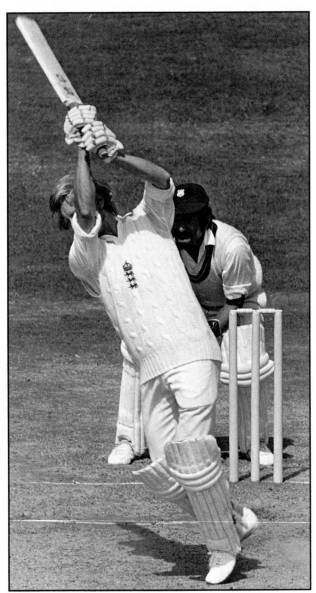

confident appeal by the West Indies against Geoff Boycott for a catch behind the wicket. Rohan Kanhai ostentatiously showed his displeasure at the decision and continued to do so for at least two hours. Fagg asked for an apology at close of play but didn't get one. So the next morning he refused to go out at the start of play and Alan Oakman took his place for one over. However after talks with the West Indian manager and Alec Bedser, Chairman of the England selectors, Fagg agreed to continue in the match. But it left a nasty taste in the mouth.

Incidentally in this Test every member of the West Indian team was a county player, which showed how widespread the influx of overseas players had become.

3. The third Test at Lord's was famous for its bomb scare which stopped play for 85 minutes while a search was made. Lord's was packed with 28,000 people on the Saturday, when soon after lunch the voice of MCC Secretary Billy Griffith announced over the public address that all the gates had been opened and that the ground must be cleared immediately. People left the ground in an orderly fashion, the West Indians went back to their nearby hotel and the England players took refuge in the hospitality tent at the back of the pavilion. (A fat lot of good that would have done them had the bomb gone off!) One or two elderly members, who had probably been asleep, resisted at first the police orders to leave the ground (below). Dickie Bird stayed out in the middle perched on one of the covers. I had been on the air when the announcement was made, and continued to broadcast for the next hour or so, trying to keep the people waiting outside the ground up to date with what was happening. We all stayed up in the commentary box right at the top of a now deserted pavilion. We hid our nerves by assuring ourselves that if the bomb did go off we at least wouldn't have so far to go!

4. The 0–2 defeat by West Indies made the selectors decide to replace Ray Illingworth as captain after 31 Tests. It was probably time for a change but he had done a good job for England since he took over the captaincy in 1969, and deservedly was awarded the CBE. His successor was Mike Denness whose first job was to take the MCC team to the West Indies, where he got off to a good start by halving the series 1–1. I no longer went on tours as BBC Cricket Correspondent but I did see the third Test in Barbados, my chief memory of it being the number of no-balls called in the match, 99 altogether with 20 of them being scored off, both sides being equally responsible.

1974

A wet and rather forgettable summer with a double tour by India and Pakistan.

England beat India easily 3–0. India's spinners, who had been so successful in 1971, had lost their touch and I think that the following figures will sum up the series.

England Batting Averages:

with Tony Greig a comparative failure with only 79.50.

David Lloyd	260·00
Keith Fletcher	189·00
John Edrich	101·50
Mike Denness	96·33
Dennis Amiss	92·50

Now look at the Indian bowling averages:
It really says it all.

Pakistan was a tougher nut and all three Tests were drawn. The first two at Headingley and Lord's were interrupted by rain, and both were low scoring games, with Underwood taking 13 wickets at Lord's, where rain seeped under the covers.

	Wickets	Av
Bedi	10	52.30
Chandrasekhar	2	63.00
Prasanna	3	89.00
Venkat	0 for 96 runs	

David Lloyd on his way to a double century at Headingley

No play was possible on the last day when England needed only 60 to win with all their wickets in hand. So but for the rain they would certainly have won, but in view of the leaking covers, it's perhaps just as well that they didn't.

The final Test at The Oval was played on perhaps too perfect a pitch. Pakistan made 600 for 7 dec. with Zaheer Abbas producing another massive score of 240. England replied with 545 which, in addition to Dennis Amiss making 183, included a new record for the slowest first-class century in England – 122 by Keith Fletcher (left). His hundred took him seven hours 38 minutes and is still the slowest Test hundred made in England.

We had at least one good laugh during the season. It was at Old Trafford against India when there was no play on the Saturday before 1 pm. At 11.25 am the announcer cued over to me on Test Match Special: '...and so to find out prospects of play – over to Brian Johnston.'

It was a miserable cold morning, and all the Indian supporters in the stand below us were huddled up in their overcoats against the weather. So I replied: 'It's raining here and there certainly won't be any play for some time yet.' I then meant to say: 'There's a dirty black cloud here.' Unfortunately what I did say was: 'There's a dirty black crowd here.' The late Maharajah of Baroda – a great friend whom we called Prince – was one of the summarisers, and luckily he laughed as loud as anyone.

1975

Nineteen seventy-five was a great summer for cricket. The sun shone, there was the first ever World Cup Tournament sponsored by Prudential, and a four Test series against Australia.

The World Cup was a great success. England was beaten by Australia in the semi-final and Australia was beaten by West Indies in the final at Lord's.

Australia won the Test series 1–0 and so kept the Ashes. In the winter I had seen Lillee and Thomson bowling at Sydney in the third Test, so knew what to expect. At the time they were the fastest and most frightening combination of fast bowlers whom I had seen since Lindwall and Miller. Once again, even on slower England pitches, they were a formidable duo and took 37 wickets between them in the four Tests.

In the first Test at Edgbaston they were helped by Mike Denness's decision to put Australia in to bat. It was a dull grey morning and the England bowlers fancied their chances and supported Denness. There was also probably a wish not to have to face Lillee and Thomson in those conditions. Anyway, it was a fatal decision, as it was England who in the end had to bat on a wet wicket. Australia won by an innings and 85 runs with a day and a half to spare, Lillee taking 5 for 15 in the first innings, and Thomson 5 for 38 in the second. Graham Gooch made a pair in his first Test, and Mike Denness was dropped as captain and replaced by Tony Greig.

Gooch caught March bowled Thomson at Edgbaston

For the Lord's Test, the selectors made an inspired choice and selected a bespectacled 33-year-old grey-haired batsman called David Steele (above). He lived up to his name. He was never intimidated, hit the bad balls and played most other balls off the front foot with a very straight bat. At Lord's he made 50 and 45, at Headingley 73 and 92 and at The Oval 39 and 66. It was a remarkable performance and he was rewarded by his local butcher who gave him a lamb chop for every run he scored plus a steak for every fifty. He had to buy an extra freezer!

1975

The Lord's game was evenly contested with Tony Greig making 96 in his first Test as captain. Ross Edwards was unlucky to be out for 99 for Australia. John Edrich then made 175, the second highest score against Australia at Lord's after Wally Hammond's 240 in 1938. After four very hot days a thunderstorm on the last day prevented England from pressing home their advantage, though Australia were never in any great trouble, and the match was drawn.

It will always be remembered as the match when a 'streaker' appeared for the first time on a Test ground (below). Luckily I was not on the air and John Arlott handled the situation with his usual wit and delicacy. Alan Knott was the non-striker and told me it was the first time he'd seen two balls coming down the pitch at the same time! After the match a friend of mine sent me the following poem:

'He ran on in his birthday attire
and set all the ladies a'fire
When he came to the stumps
he misjudged his jumps
Now he sings in the Luton Girls' Choir!'

The third Test at Headingley was evenly balanced before the last day. But during the night vandals damaged the pitch (below),

and the match had to be abandoned. As it happened heavy rain would have stopped it anyway. The best bowling for England was by Phil Edmonds (above) *who in his first Test took 5 for 28 but was badly mauled in the second innings taking only 1 wicket for 64 runs.*

The final Test at The Oval was the longest Test ever played in England. It lasted six days and ended as late as 3rd September – the first time I had commentated on a Test match in September.

It was a high-scoring match with McCosker (127) and Ian Chappell (192) making more than half of Australia's 532. England made only 191 but when they followed on, Bob Woolmer who had been dropped at Leeds, played a match-saving innings of 149. He took six hours 34 minutes to reach his hundred – then the slowest ever by an Englishman against Australia.

There were two quite amusing incidents during the match. Whilst he was batting in the first innings, John Snow tried all he could to hint to the umpires that the light was bad. But when they disregarded his long glances up at the dark clouds he suddenly got fed up and hit Max Walker for 4 over mid-off, then gave him the charge and lofted him over long-on for another 4, and finally played a cross batted stroke for 2. Ten runs off the over, the most expensive of the day. At the end of it the umpires conferred and decided the light was too bad to continue. I wonder how many Snow would have made if the light had been good!

The other thing which amused me but possibly no one else was when Trevor Bailey was discussing whether England should have taken more risks to score more quickly in their second innings. 'It's very difficult to strike a happy medium,' he said. 'You could go to a seance,' I butted in, to the groans of my colleagues in the box.

1976

This was one of the best summers ever. The sun shone throughout, and a spell of fifteen days in June and July was the hottest and longest over the previous two hundred and fifty years.

The West Indies had one of its strongest sides, and under Clive Lloyd won the series easily, 3–0. There was a batting order of magnificent stroke-players: Fredericks, Greenidge, Richards, Kallicharran, Lloyd and King. They were supported by a frightening trio of fast bowlers: Roberts, Holding and Daniel.

The first Test at Trent Bridge was drawn in spite of a masterly 232 by Viv Richards (left). He was then only 24 years old and at the peak of his power. He undoubtedly has a touch of genius but is not a batsman for schoolboys to copy. Although he has strokes all round the wicket he favours the on-side, often playing across the line of the ball. His speciality has been to hit balls outside the off-stump over square leg for six!

England was able to draw the match thanks to David Steele continuing his 1975 form with 106.

Lord's was another draw and might have been won by England had not Saturday been completely washed-out and not a ball bowled, with the gates closed at 10.40 am and with thousands locked outside. This was the only black mark for the weather during the summer. It spoilt an even match. At the close West Indies, set 323 to win, were 241 for 6 with all their top six batsmen out.

The West Indies won the third test at Old Trafford easily by 425 runs with a century in each innings by Gordon Greenidge (opposite, above) and another one by Viv Richards. But for me the match was spoilt by some of the most vicious and hostile fast bowling I have ever seen. In the first innings England collapsed for 71, only David Steele (20) reaching double figures. Andy Roberts with 3 wickets, Michael Holding with 5 and Wayne Daniel with 2 were the destroyers. West Indies players themselves, in spite of Greenidge, had only made 211 so batted again and declared at 411 for 5 soon after tea on the third day. It was then that John Edrich, aged 39, and Brian Close (opposite, below) aged 45, were subjected to an unacceptable barrage of bouncers which Clive Lloyd, the West Indian captain, seemed actively to encourage. I'm afraid, too, that the umpires did little to stop it until Bill Alley belatedly warned Holding towards the end of the 80 minutes which Edrich and Close had to endure. They were both renowned for their courage, and needed it as they defended bravely with bat and body, without caring about runs.

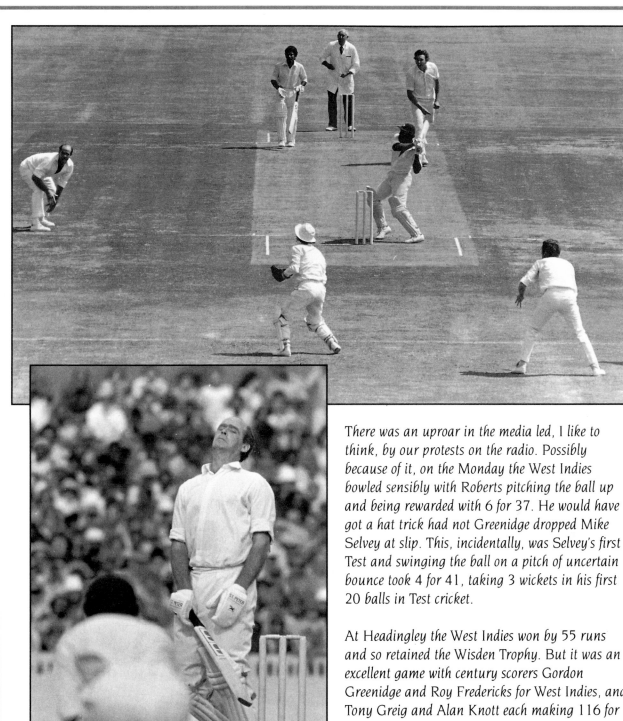

There was an uproar in the media led, I like to think, by our protests on the radio. Possibly because of it, on the Monday the West Indies bowled sensibly with Roberts pitching the ball up and being rewarded with 6 for 37. He would have got a hat trick had not Greenidge dropped Mike Selvey at slip. This, incidentally, was Selvey's first Test and swinging the ball on a pitch of uncertain bounce took 4 for 41, taking 3 wickets in his first 20 balls in Test cricket.

At Headingley the West Indies won by 55 runs and so retained the Wisden Trophy. But it was an excellent game with century scorers Gordon Greenidge and Roy Fredericks for West Indies, and Tony Greig and Alan Knott each making 116 for England. All the fast bowlers on both sides did well, Underwood for once not taking a single wicket.

There were several outstanding features of the fifth Test at The Oval which the West Indies won by 231 runs.

1. There was a majestic exhibition of batting by Viv Richards who made 291 out of the West Indies total of 687 for 8 dec. We were all betting that he would pass Len Hutton's 364, the highest individual Test score at The Oval, and of course Gary Sobers's 365 not out which became the record in 1958. But he naturally began to tire and played on to Tony Greig.

2. There was a tremendously brave come-back by Dennis Amiss (above) who made a magnificent 203. Earlier in the season, playing for MCC against the West Indies at Lord's, he had ducked to a very fast ball from Michael Holding which struck him on the back of the head, and he had to go to hospital. I saw it all from sideways on and I must say that Holding's speed that evening was such that you couldn't follow the ball through the air. But now brought back for the fifth Test – he hadn't played in any of the others – Amiss bravely stood up to the fast bowling for over seven hours and hit 28 fours. But even he was overshadowed by Michael Holding (opposite) who, on a slowish pitch unhelpful to fast bowling, took 8 for 92 and 6 for 57 in the match. It was beautiful to watch. He took a long run of about 25 yards and seemed to float on the air as he glided like a gazelle over the turf. It was said that the umpires never heard him coming. He was nicknamed 'Whispering Death', and someone aptly said that he could run on soft snow without leaving a footprint. I know Trevor Bailey thinks this was the best fast bowling he had ever seen on such an unhelpful wicket, and I am happy to agree with him.

1976

There was an amusing incident in the Oval Test as a result of my constant urging of Knotty to stand up to the medium pace bowlers. When he asked me to write a piece for his benefit brochure I said I would do so – but at a price. He must promise to stand up to the slow medium Bob Woolmer when he came on to bowl. Sure enough when Woolmer was put on Knotty immediately went and stood up close behind the stumps (below), *giving a thumbs up to me in the commentary box as he did so.* Next door our TV colleagues were speculating whether this was some ruse for a leg side stumping. The left-handed Fredericks was the batsman and to my horror Woolmer's first ball was miles outside the leg stump. I thought, oh my goodness there go four byes. But Knotty of course took it brilliantly. When Woolmer began his second over, Knotty having paid for my article, went and stood back to him. Its nice to think that this sort of thing can go on even in the serious atmosphere of a Test Match.

The Queen's Jubilee year was somewhat wetter than 1976! In March, following England's tour of India, there was the Centenary Test in Melbourne. It was a great occasion with 200 old Test players present. Unfortunately, due to Down your Way, I myself was not able to go. By a strange coincidence, Australia won by exactly the same number of runs – 45 – as they had won by in 1877.

During the summer, England regained the Ashes beating the old enemy 3–0. But before that happened there came the shock revelation in May that Kerry Packer had signed up 35 Test players from England, Australia, West Indies, South Africa and Pakistan. It shook the cricket world which had lived in cuckoo-land for too long, the players being grossly underpaid. So change was inevitable but most people regretted the underhand way in which it had all been carried out. Even during the tour of India and during the Centenary match itself, Tony Greig, captain of England, was involved in the secret plot which would rob both England and Australia of Test cricketers in the future. It cast a blight over the season, and must have affected the form and team spirit of both sides.

Still, there were many worthwhile achievements.

Mike Brearley (seen below talking to the press), began his reign as England's captain after Tony Greig had been sacked. The first Test, unusually, was played at Lords to celebrate the Queen's Jubilee. Nearly six hours were lost because of rain, and it was drawn. For England Bob Woolmer made 79 and 120, and Bob Willis bowled at his fastest to take 7 for 78 in Australia's first innings, and took 27 wickets in the series.

1977

For Australia the fast slinger Jeff Thomson (opposite) was as fast as ever, and took 8 wickets in this Test and 23 in the series.

In the second Test at Old Trafford Bob Woolmer made his second successive hundred, and Derek Underwood took 6 for 66 to help England to win by 9 wickets, in spite of a model 112 by Greg Chappell – the only class batsman in his side.

England won again at Trent Bridge by 7 wickets. The match produced some notable events. Geoff Boycott, after a self-imposed exile of three years from Test cricket, returned in place of Amiss to partner Brearley. Typically, he made the most of it by making 107, though in the process he ran out the local hero Derek Randall (below, right), and had to be nursed along and encouraged by Alan Knott who played in his usual cheeky fashion for 135, and became the first Test wicket-keeper to make 4000 runs.

It was also the first Test of a young 21-year-old all-rounder called Ian Botham. He got off to a great start taking 5 wickets in Australia's first innings.

It seemed as if Boycott (below) might surpass himself and make two hundreds in the match, but he was only 80 not out when England won.

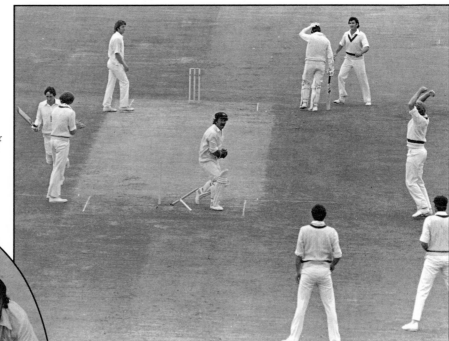

His 107 had been his ninety-eighth hundred, and in the only match in which he played before the next Test at Headingley, he made his ninety-ninth for Yorkshire against Warwickshire.

So the stage was all set for him to get his hundredth hundred before his home crowd at Headingley, and of course he obliged to tremendous acclaim with a great innings of 191. He helped England to 436 and Australia was beaten by an innings for England to regain the Ashes.

1977

This should have been the highlight of the match and, although Derek Randall turned a cart-wheel in celebration (right), the Yorkshire crowd could only call for Boycott — the Ashes were forgotten. Incidentally, Ian Botham continued on his way with another bag of 5 wickets in Australia's first innings (below).

England had been astutely captained by Brearley and the bowling, led by Mike Hendrick (8 wickets in the match), was steady and accurate.

The drawn fifth Test at The Oval was an anti-climax ruined by rain.

The cricket was fairly uneventful – England under Mike Brearley beating Pakistan 2–0, and New Zealand 3–0. Neither of the visiting teams put up any outstanding performances.

For England Ian Botham continued merrily on his way making two hundreds and taking 13 wickets against Pakistan, and taking 24 wickets against New Zealand.

There were several firsts:

1. For the first time – on the 1977–78 tour of Pakistan – the touring team was called England and not MCC. This in some ways was a sad break with tradition, and indeed overseas it seemed to be generally regretted. But it was a logical move since the TCCB and not MCC now selected the team and ran the tours.

Botham running out Hadlee at Lord's

2. Nineteen seventy-eight was the first year of Cornhill Insurance sponsoring Test cricket. It is still going strong in 1990 and has benefited the counties, the players and also Cornhill itself. The players are now far better paid. What a pity it took Kerry Packer to make this happen. The counties have also received vastly improved contributions from the TCCB.

3. The first Test against Pakistan at Edgbaston was the first of David Gower's 109 Tests and he scored a four off the first ball he received. It was a short one on the leg-side from Liaquat Ali, and David nonchalantly pulled it round to backward square leg for four (below). 7862 Test runs later he still plays the same way, on his day very very well, and on his occasional bad day, very very badly. He is a 'touch' player depending on his timing, and has always been vulnerable off his legs to a leg slip, or from outside his off stump to the slips or the gully. It wouldn't be Gower if he didn't take risks and sometimes appear like ordinary mortals. But he has brought elegance, grace, good manners and sportsmanship to Test cricket. Laid back and seemingly casual? Yes, but underneath it all there has been plenty of steel. You don't make 7000 Test runs against all the world's top bowlers without it.

The World Cup tournament took place in England. It was won for the second time by the West Indies; who beat England in the final at Lord's, largely due to an exciting partnership of 139 between Viv Richards (138 not out) and Collis King (86).

Four Tests against India followed, England winning the first and the other three being drawn. Gavaskar for India and Boycott and Gower for England were the outstanding batsmen. In the first Test at Edgbaston which England won by an innings and 83 runs, Gower (below left) made 200 not out, his first double century in first-class cricket. Boycott made 155 to reach 6000 runs in Test cricket, and this meant that he had scored a Test hundred on each of England's six Test grounds. Botham took 5 wickets in India's second innings and followed this up in the second Test at Lord's with another 5 in India's first innings. They were all out 96 but saved the match thanks to a hundred each by Vengsarkar (below right) and the diminutive Viswanath (overleaf, top left) in their second innings, in an entertaining but frustrating partnership from England's point of view.

Only just over 11½ hours' play was possible in the third Test at Headingley, though there was time for Botham to make a spectacular 137 with 5 sixes and 16 fours.

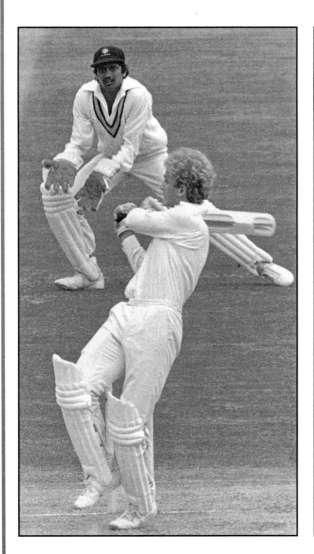

1979

So India still had a chance of squaring the series if they won the last Test at The Oval. And they came miraculously near to doing so in a really thrilling finish.

They were set 438 runs to win in 498 minutes and thanks to a superb 221 by 'Sunny' Gavaskar (above right) they needed 15 runs off the last over with two wickets in hand. They got 6 of them in one of the most gallant recoveries I have ever seen, ending with 429 for 8.

It's difficult to keep Botham (right) out of any chronicle of the Test Matches in this era. Besides taking 20 wickets in the series, he also reached 1000 runs in Test cricket. With his 107 wickets this meant that at the age of twenty-three in only 21 Tests he had reached his Test double in two Tests fewer than the previous record held by Vinoo Mankad.

*I*an Botham (right, tossing up with Clive Lloyd) took over the England captaincy from Mike Brearley. West Indies won the five Test series 1–0, rain interfering with the other four which were all draws. Once again they employed bouncers and a slow over rate, and Joel Garner, Andy Roberts, Michael Holding and Malcolm Marshall were a fearsome quartet. But with their long run-ups and slow walk-backs the spectators were robbed of a lot of cricket.

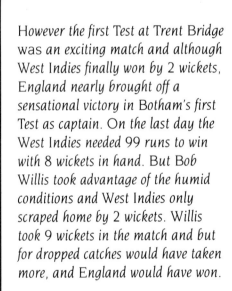

However the first Test at Trent Bridge was an exciting match and although West Indies finally won by 2 wickets, England nearly brought off a sensational victory in Botham's first Test as captain. On the last day the West Indies needed 99 runs to win with 8 wickets in hand. But Bob Willis took advantage of the humid conditions and West Indies only scraped home by 2 wickets. Willis took 9 wickets in the match and but for dropped catches would have taken more, and England would have won.

The second Test at Lord's produced some fine batting. Graham Gooch (123), driving powerfully, scored his first Test century (left), and Desmond Haynes (184) and Viv Richards (145) put on 223 for the second wicket, with Richards in his first Test at Lord's in particularly sparkling form.

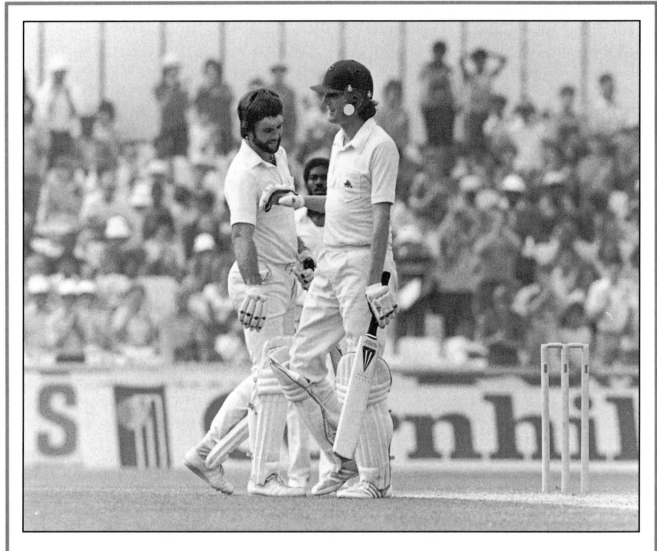

Peter Willey played quite a part in the next two Tests. At Old Trafford he made a fighting 62 not out. At The Oval he made 100 not out, and with Bob Willis put on 117 runs for the last wicket (above, Willey without helmet).

He was also concerned in one of my gaffes which I did not know I had made at the time. After the match I received a letter from a lady who said how much she had enjoyed my commentary at The Oval, but as there were many young people listening to Test Match Special, I should be more careful in what I said. Did I realise that when Michael Holding was bowling to Peter Willey I had said: 'And now the bowler's Holding, the batsman's Willey'?

In 1880 at The Oval England and Australia had played their first Test in England. One hundred years later a Centenary match was played at Lord's in celebration, Australia making a special visit to this country for it.

Off the field it was a great success, with over two hundred former Test players from both countries being present. It was a highly successful social occasion. But rain interfered with the cricket and ten hours were lost on the first three days. On the Saturday in brilliant sunshine and with a 20,000 crowd there was no play possible until late in the afternoon because of the wet state of the ground. It was rumoured that the ground staff thought play could have started earlier, but the two umpires Dickie Bird and David Constant thought not. If this had been a normal Test Match, they were probably right. But this was a very special occasion and the captains Ian Botham and Kim Hughes are equally to blame. They could have overruled the umpires and have said that they both wanted to play.

All this led to some frustrated members of MCC booing and jostling the umpires, David Constant actually being struck by a member. It was all a great pity. Believe it or not, when play finally started at 3.45 pm the umpires had a police escort through the Long Room. What would Lord Harris have said?

Australia had far the better of the cricket, Kim Hughes (below) playing two delightful innings of 117 and 84 using his feet and attacking all the bowlers. He declared both his innings and England, dismissed for 205 in the first innings, were asked to get 370 to win in about six hours, or roughly a run a minute. Thanks to Boycott (128 not out) they never looked like losing, but again, because this was a special occasion, I felt that Ian Botham should have instructed his batsmen to go for victory – or even have come in earlier himself. It would have shown good intentions. As it was, the match petered out into a dull draw with England 244 for 3. A sad ending to the otherwise successful Centenary celebration.

1980

One puzzling memory of 1980 was when Geoff Boycott came on to bowl in the second Test at Lord's. He bowled in his cap (opposite), putting it on back to front just like the motor-cyclists used to do before they wore helmets. I have never asked him why he did it, but it was a strange thing to do.

2nd September, 1980,

at Lord's was a sad day for Test Match Special. After 35 years in which he covered every Test played in this country, John Arlott said his farewell from the commentary box (above). He had been fêted round the Test Match circuit all through the summer, and he must have eaten — and drunk! — a record number of farewell dinners. At Lord's on the last day our box was full of TV and newspaper cameramen as John was shot time and time again at the microphone. His last spell usually finished at about 3 pm when he then went off to write his piece for The Guardian. We were all gathered in the box expecting him to give a short speech of thanks and to say goodbye to the millions of listeners all over the world who loved his wit and Hampshire burr. But no, as he described the last ball of the over he just gave the score and said: 'And after a word from Trevor Bailey, it will be Christopher Martin-Jenkins.' Just that, nothing more, though there was a slight break in his voice. We all applauded as he got up and left the box, and made his way past the members clapping him as he disappeared down the stairs. Luckily Alan Curtis on the public address announced to the crowd that John Arlott had just completed his final broadcast for the BBC. The crowd all stood and cheered and so did the Australians on the field. It was a moving moment and a well deserved tribute from everyone at the headquarters of cricket.

1981

Botham's year. This was the year of the two big turn-arounds, first in Ian Botham's career and secondly in the amazing Headingley Test.

Botham's captaincy had not been much of a success: 12 Tests; Won 0, Lost 4, Drawn 8. I for one had always believed it was asking too much of him to take on the captaincy plus doing so much else.

He bowled as many overs, sometimes more, than the regular bowlers. He fielded at second slip which calls for continual concentration. And whenever he batted there was always great expectation from the crowds. It was bound to affect his cricket if he had to have all the extra worry and reponsibility of captaincy. And it did, the final straw coming in the second Test against Australia at Lord's. In the first Test at Trent Bridge Australia won by 4 wickets, and Bob Willis (below) took his 200th wicket for England. For Australia Rodney Marsh passed Alan Knott's total of 244 Test match catches. In addition, Trevor Chappell joined his brothers Ian and Greg as a Test cricketer, the only three Australian brothers to do so.

Botham retires to the pavilion after collecting a pair at Lord's.

In the drawn Lord's Test Botham made a pair and immediately after he had returned to the pavilion he told Alec Bedser, Chairman of Selectors, that he resigned the captaincy. It's fair to say that if he hadn't, Bedser was about to tell him that he was being dropped as captain by the selectors. As I said, although Botham himself denied it, and always wanted to be captain, his form was badly affected. In the twelve Tests in which he was captain he scored 276 runs at an average of 13.14, and his 35 wickets were expensive at 33 runs apiece.

Mike Brearley was recalled to captain England and both England's and Botham's fortunes changed miraculously for the better. The next three Tests were like fairy stories. At Headingley at first everything seemed to go wrong for Mike Brearley. Although Botham took 6 wickets, Australia made 401 for 9 dec. and against Lillee and Alderman England only made 174 (Botham 50!) so had to follow on 227 runs behind and were immediately in trouble again against Lillee and Alderman. They were 135 for 7 when Graham Dilley who batted left-handed and had never made 50 joined Botham. They soon decided they might as well enjoy themselves and give it 'oompty'. And it came off. They put on 117 in 80 minutes, before Dilley was out for 56. Chris Old made an invaluable 29 and Bob Willis added 37 with Botham who finished with an amazing 149 not out. His hundred came off only 87 balls and he had hit the Australian bowlers to all parts of the field with cuts, hooks (opposite, top) and hefty drives . Even so when Willis was out, Australia only needed 130 to win.

Botham got the first wicket bowling downhill and down wind from the Kirkstall Lane end. After 7 overs he was replaced by Willis who had been trundling uphill and up wind from the Football Stand end. I asked him afterwards why he, the fastest bowler, should have had to do that. He replied that he had thought the same thing, and asked Brearley why he had put him on at that end. 'To make you angry,' was Brearley's reply. And my goodness how it worked! I have never seen Willis more het up and bowling at such a ferocious pace. He took 8 for 43, his best ever Test figures, and England had beaten Australia in this remarkable topsy-turvy match, by 18 runs.

This victory seemed to inspire the team, and became the talk of England. Cricket was front page news. It was too much to expect another miracle at Edgbaston but it happened after Australia had once again been set a small target to win, just 151. They were doing well enough at 105 for 4 but then lost their last 6 wickets for 16 runs and England had won by 29 runs. And the cause of their collapse? Botham of course! He had only taken 1 for 64 in the first innings, and none so far in the second innings. He was looking rather out of sorts and seemed reluctant to bowl. But Brearley cajoled him into action and he proceeded to take 5 wickets for 1 run in 28 balls. Even though it took place on a Sunday, it was still unbelievable.

Not even Botham could walk on water forever, and true enough he made 0 in England's first innings at Old Trafford. He half made up for this by taking 3 wickets and aided by Willis (4) and Allott (2) bowled out

Australia for 130 giving England a lead of 101. Fine bowling by Alderman (left) reduced England to 104 for 5 when Botham strode in to play what I'm sure he feels is his finest Test innings, and was undoubtedly the best that many of those at Old Trafford had ever seen. He reached his hundred this time in only 86 balls, and his six sixes (opposite) are a record for any Test innings in England. In addition he hit 13 fours, and for once built up his innings slowly, taking 67 minutes over his first 28 runs.

But then Australia took the new ball and his next 66 runs came off only 8 overs. His hooking of Lillee off his eyebrows was brave and spectacular and three sixes sailed over long leg.

Of course once again he was the hero of every small boy in England, but two unsung heroes helped England to win by 103. Paul Allott playing in his first Test on his home ground, not only took 4 wickets in the match, but copied Dilley and also made his first first-class fifty – 52 not out.

Chris Tavaré was the other hero. He didn't get much applause from the crowd but how valuable was his second innings of 78. He helped Botham put on 149 for the 6th wicket, and batted for seven hours scoring the slowest ever fifty in English first-class cricket. He looked impregnable, barely lifting his bat more than an inch or so off the ground.

With England leading in the series 3–1, the sixth Test at The Oval was inevitably an anti-climax. Centuries by Alan Border and Dick Welham for Australia, and one by Geoff Boycott were the batting highlights. In bowling Lillee again bowled magnificently taking 11 wickets to give him 39 in the series. But he was pipped by Alderman who in his first ever six Tests took 42 wickets with his accurate swing bowling. Oh yes, I forgot, a certain gentleman called Ian Botham took 10 wickets to give him 34 in the series. Close behind was Bob Willis with 29.

It was a year I shall never forget, and was a terrific boost for cricket.

1982

The visitors were India and Pakistan on another of their shared tours. England beat India 1–0, and Pakistan 2–1. India's batting was stronger than their bowling, a fine 157 at Lord's by Vengsarkar particularly caught the eye.

Another batsman to do well was S.M. Patil (right) at Old Trafford where he hit 129 not out and set a world record by hitting Willis for six fours in one over, which incidentally contained seven deliveries, as one was a no-ball.

Bob Willis took over the captaincy of England from Keith Fletcher, dropped after his unsuccessful tour of India in the winter of 1981–82. Willis was England's best bowler taking 15 wickets with his speed and often uncomfortable lift. But even so, India managed innings of 369, 379 and 410.

At The Oval Ian Botham scored one of the fastest double centuries (208) ever scored by an England batsman. He reached his 200 off only 220 balls and hit four sixes and 19 fours, one of the sixes making a hole in the pavilion roof.

Pakistan, led by the charismatic Imran Khan (opposite above), was a better side than India. Although losing the first and third Tests, Pakistan outplayed England at Lord's and won by 10 wickets, just beating the weather to score the 77 runs needed – only their second ever victory over England. Mohsin Khan played a delightful innings of 200 exactly, with some lovely drives through the covers.

It was a joy to see Abdul Qadir (left) bowling his leg spin and googlies, of which he boasted he could bowl three different varieties. The England

batsmen always seemed unhappy against him but strangely enough except in the first innings at Lord's (4 for 39), he was usually expensive and only took 10 wickets in the series at a cost of 40.60 apiece. But what fun he was to watch, as he licked his fingers before starting on his short angled run with arms twirling. Imran himself was by far the best bowler, fast and accurate, and took 21 wickets in the series besides averaging over 50 with the bat.

In the Lord's Test David Gower captained England as Bob Willis had wricked his neck avoiding a bouncer in the first Test!

On a personal note, the first day of the second Test v. India at Old Trafford was a highlight for me.

The BBC really went to town to celebrate my seventieth birthday. They gave a champagne breakfast for me at the hotel in which we always stay at Bucklow Hill (below). In the evening they gave a dinner in my honour at the BBC in Manchester.

This was preceded by an 'internal' This Is Your Life conducted by Christopher Martin-Jenkins with Eamonn Andrews' voice and inflections taken off to perfection. In the true tradition of the real show, it ended with Jenkers saying: 'you thought your wife Pauline and daughter Clare were in your home in St John's Wood. But tonight we've flown them 190 miles up here to be with you on this happy occasion', and to my genuine surprise in stepped my wife and daughter. A very happy climax to what had been a lovely sunny day — capped by a quick 50 by Ian Botham off only 46 balls, and including ten fours. An exhilarating birthday present.

<u>Australia</u>

I went out to Sydney after Christmas to see our son Andrew, and of course the fifth and final Test between England and Australia, the latter leading 2–1. On this tour the BBC, under Peter Baxter, set up its own Test Match Special, and used any of us who were available. As I was in Sydney I naturally joined the team and it was nice to broadcast a Test Match again from Sydney. The last time I had been there on the air was in 1971 when Ray Illingworth's team regained the Ashes.

England needed to win to square the series but could only manage a draw, so it was Australia's turn to regain the Ashes.

There was one unfortunate decision by one of the umpires off the last ball of Bob Willis's first over. Without a run on the board he appeared to have thrown out Dyson. But Dyson was given not out, although when the action replay was shown on a large screen on the ground, Dyson was shown to be at least a foot if not more short of the crease. He went on to make 79, so it must have had quite an effect on the match. I personally am strongly against showing the action replay to the crowd. It puts the umpire in an impossible position if he has made a mistake – and we all do that.

Eddie Hemmings (right) came into the side as the Sydney wicket usually takes spin at some time in a five-day match. Sure enough, he took 6 wickets but even better made a gallant 95 after being sent in as night-watchman on the fourth evening. It was rotten luck that he didn't get his first Test hundred, but he did save England from possible defeat.

My happiest memory of the match was on second day, when I was busy commentating, and a message came up the line from England saying my daughter Clare had just presented me with my first grandchild. Andrew quickly 'achieved' some champagne (right) and our commentary was interrupted by a few celebratory popping of corks.

Since his birth was announced over the air during a Test Match, it is perhaps appropriate that Nicholas, at the age of seven, looks as if he will be a fine left-hand bat and a fast right-arm Procter-like bowler.

The third Prudential World Cup was surprisingly won by India. Their medium-pace bowlers were more effective on a Lord's pitch which helped seamers, than the fast bowling of the West Indies.

New Zealand, well led by Geoff Howarth, lost the four Test series 1–3, but their one victory at Lord's was their first ever against England in England. The main feature of their tour was the all-round form of Richard Hadlee (left), who off his short run seemed very fast and hostile, and with his accuracy, change of pace and late swing took 21 wickets at 26.16. He also averaged 50.61 with his attacking left-handed batting.

For England, David Gower and Alan Lamb with two hundreds apiece were the most successful batsmen, well supported by Chris Tavaré.

Bob Willis, with another 20 in this series, took his total of Test wickets to 305, the fourth bowler to pass the magic 300 mark. It was a tremendous tribute to his strength of character and determination in his daily efforts to reach peak fitness.

1984

This summer was a great triumph for the West Indies under Clive Lloyd. They made a clean sweep of the series, winning all five Tests, something no other touring side had ever done in England. They were a formidable team with their usual quota of hostile fast bowlers: Joel Garner (opposite), 6 feet 8 inches tall bringing the ball down from a great height and very difficult to score off, (29 wickets). Malcolm Marshall (overleaf above), smaller but faster with his sprint up to the wicket, whippy action and the ball skidding through, (24 wickets). Michael Holding (overleaf below), with his smooth gliding run up, now aged 30 but still the complete bowler. Even when he bowled off a shorter run, as he often did on this tour, he seemed nearly as fast as ever, (15 wickets). In support was a tall off-spinner, Roger Harper, (13 wickets) who was one of the best ever fieldsmen, matching Colin Bland for his speed and throwing.

The BBC Radio commentary team in 1984.
Back row from left: Tony Lewis, Henry Blofeld, Ray Illingworth, Christopher Martin-Jenkins, Peter Baxter, Bill Frindall.
Front row from left: Don Mosey, Trevor Bailey, myself, Fred Trueman, Tony Cozier

The batting line-up was just as strong. Gordon Greenidge (opposite, top left) and Larry Gomes both made two hundreds and averaged over 80. Clive Lloyd, Viv Richards and Desmond Haynes all played a most productive second fiddle. Gordon Greenidge achieved a Bradman-like feat, scoring two double centuries, one at Lord's, the other at Old Trafford, emulating Viv Richards who had also scored two double centuries in 1976.

What about poor old England captained by David Gower in his first full series? The best performer was undoubtedly Allan Lamb (above, right) who scored three successive hundreds at Lord's, Headingley and Old Trafford. Ian Botham, as ever, did well with both bat and ball (347 runs and 19 wickets).

It was good to see Pat Pocock, (right) now aged 37, recalled to Test Cricket at Old Trafford after eight years' absence. He brought a smile into the cricket which for my liking was far too serious, and win-at-all-costs. He had a long bowl of 45 overs and picked up 4 wickets for 121 runs with his flighty off-spin. He wasn't quite so successful with the bat, making a pair. He was selected again for the last Test at The Oval, where he achieved some sort of record by making another pair!

1984

There is a good story about the first of these two at The Oval. England, thanks to Ian Botham, Paul Allott and Richard Ellison, playing in his first Test, had bowled West Indies out for 190, and towards the end of the day Graeme Fowler and Chris Broad had to go in to open for England. Whether he lost the toss or not I don't know but poor Pat was selected by David Gower as night-watchman. He disappeared from the dressing-room and there was a rapid search for him when Broad was bowled by Garner for 4. They found Pat in the downstair wash-room below the dressing-room. He was busy gargling. When asked what he was doing he replied: 'Oh, I'm just freshening up my mouth in case Bernie Thomas has to give me the kiss of life.'

Anyway, he went in and played out time, and next morning batted bravely without scoring for three quarters of an hour against some unpleasantly fast and short pitched bowling by Malcolm Marshall. So it was really a most distinguished 0!

With so much fast bowling there was inevitably a number of injuries, and sadly two young batsmen both playing in their first season for England were seriously hurt. At Edgbaston in the first Test Andy Lloyd, opening for England, was struck on his helmet near his temple by a rising ball from Marshall (above). He had to retire with blurred vision and in fact did not play again that summer. At Old Trafford Paul Terry, playing in his second Test, was struck by a ball which fractured his left forearm. He bravely returned to try to help England save the follow-on. His left arm was in a sling under his sweater and he joined Allan Lamb who was 98 not out. Allan thought Paul had been sent out so that he could get his hundred, and off the last ball of the over ran two, instead of a single. It meant that he got his hundred but poor Paul had to face Garner, with one hand. He lasted one ball and was then bowled. He really should not have been sent in by Gower in the state he was, although England needed 23 runs to save the follow-on. I suppose if Allan had nursed Paul properly, England might just have saved it.

An even more remarkable injury story concerned Malcolm Marshall. On the first day at Headingley he suffered a double fracture of his left thumb, trying to stop a shot from Chris Broad in the gully. He was told not to play for at least ten days but amazingly appeared at No. 11 to help Larry Gomes who was 96 not out, reach his hundred. He batted one-handed (below), and if my memory is right actually hit a four. Anyway, he stayed long enough for Gomes to make 104 not out. But that is not the end of the story. Marshall, with his left hand in plaster, bowled at his fastest and fiercest in England's second innings and actually took 7 for 53, then his best bowling figures in Test cricket.

1984

Sri Lanka were touring England and at the end of August played their first ever Test in England at Lord's. We all thought that this was the chance for England to redeem her disastrous summer. But nothing seemed to go right for David Gower in 1984. He won the toss, put Sri Lanka in, and they declared at 491 for 7 with Sidath Wettimuny (right) making 190 in ten hours 36 minutes, the longest ever Test innings at Lord's. Duleep Mendis made 111 and England's bowlers were in disarray. Their batting was not much better and had Allan Lamb not been missed behind the wicket when 36, England might well have had to follow on. As it was, Lamb made his fourth Test hundred of the summer (107) and Chris Broad played solidly for 86. But it was a pathetic and shame-making performance by England. Believe it or not, on the Saturday between lunch and tea they added a mere 49 runs off 27 overs, Chris Tavaré and Chris Broad being the villains of the piece. It really was awful to watch and especially to try to commentate on. There was yet another hundred and a second declaration when Sri Lanka batted again, Silva making 102 not out and Mendis nearly scoring two hundreds in the match with 94. When Sri Lanka declared at 294 for 7 there was luckily no time for England to bat again!

During the Sri Lanka second innings, Botham (6 for 90) passed Lance Gibbs (309) and Freddie Trueman (307) to take his total of Test wickets to 312.

It really had been a disastrous summer for English cricket.

What a contrast to the depressing summer of 1984. And what a change in the fortunes of England and their captain David Gower. Not only did England beat Australia 3–1 but David himself averaged 81.33 and made 732 runs – 200 more than the next best scorer, Mike Gatting, who made 527 runs at an average of 87.83. Mike made two hundreds, David three, including 215, his highest score in Test cricket.

There were several reasons for England's improved form. First and foremost Australia were not a good side. Their selection had been hampered by some of their best players such as Kim Hughes, Terry Alderman, Graham Yallop and Rodney Hogg opting to go on a tour of South Africa, and so making themselves unavailable. There was also a certain amount of internal strife within the team, largely because some of them had changed their minds about going to South Africa at the last moment, and the 'loyalists' in the team thought that they should not have been chosen.

In spite of this, their captain Allan Border (left) had a wonderful tour with the bat. He scored 597 runs in the Tests, averaging 66.33 and scoring two hundreds. None of the other batsmen were outstanding, although Greg Ritchie showed promise with stylish innings at Lord's, Trent Bridge and The Oval.

Allan Border was transformed from the unexciting player we had seen in 1980 and 1981. He now used his feet and seemed to have a penchant for hitting sixes. In addition to his Test performances he started off the tour with four successive hundreds.

1985

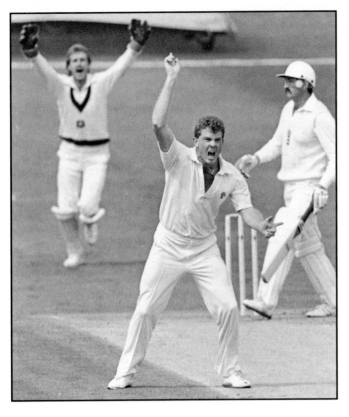

The other big success for Australia was Craig McDermott (left), a 20 year old. He was fast and strong with a fiery temperament, though obviously inexperienced. But still he took 30 wickets in the six Tests, though they cost 30.03 each.

It was a wettish summer but the rain did not interfere too badly with the Tests. In fact, remarkably, because the wickets were inevitably on the slow side, that rate of scoring was unbelievably fast for Test cricket, England averaging over 60 runs per 100 balls. In addition to Gower and Gatting, Tim Robinson and Graham Gooch each scored nearly 500 runs. Ian Botham, after the first two Tests was, as a batsman, rather out of the limelight. But his 60 in 51 balls at Headingley and a steady (for him!) 85 at Lord's helped England to win the first Test, but could not prevent Australia winning the second. But you can't keep a good man down and as a bowler Ian took 31 wickets, and at Lord's passed Bob Willis's 325 wickets in Tests. I cannot resist adding that in all first-class cricket in 1985 Ian averaged 69.54 and hit 80 sixes, a record for any English season.

In these days of medium-fast bowlers plugging away, it was a personal pleasure for me to be able to commentate on two types of bowlers now all too rarely seen: the genuine outswinger and the leg-break bowler. Richard Ellison only played in the last two Tests and proved how difficult the outswinger can be to play. His analysis for the two Tests was:

75.5–20–185–17–10.88

Not bad figures!

Bob Holland was Australia's leg-spinner. He had his day of triumph in England's second innings at Lord's, where bowling round the wicket into the rough he took 5 for 68, in his first appearance in Test in England.

Nineteen eighty-five will always be David Gower's golden summer. He also caught a most unusual catch at Edgbaston, which prevented Australia saving the match and caused a bit of controversy at the time. Wayne Phillips, the left-handed wicket-keeper, was bravely trying to stop the rot in Australia's second innings. When he came in they were 36 for 5, and when he had made 59 and Australia had recovered to 113 for 5, he hit a ball from Phil Edmonds hard to Allan Lamb at silly point. Allan tried to get out of the way but the ball hit him painfully on the instep from where it rebounded to Gower who caught it at silly mid-off (opposite). David Shepherd had been unsighted but checked with David Constant at square leg who had no hesitation in giving Phillips out. The Australians, especially Allan Border, were not too happy, alleging that the ball had hit the ground. But the action replay on TV, and the bruise on Lamb's instep proved that they were wrong!

1985

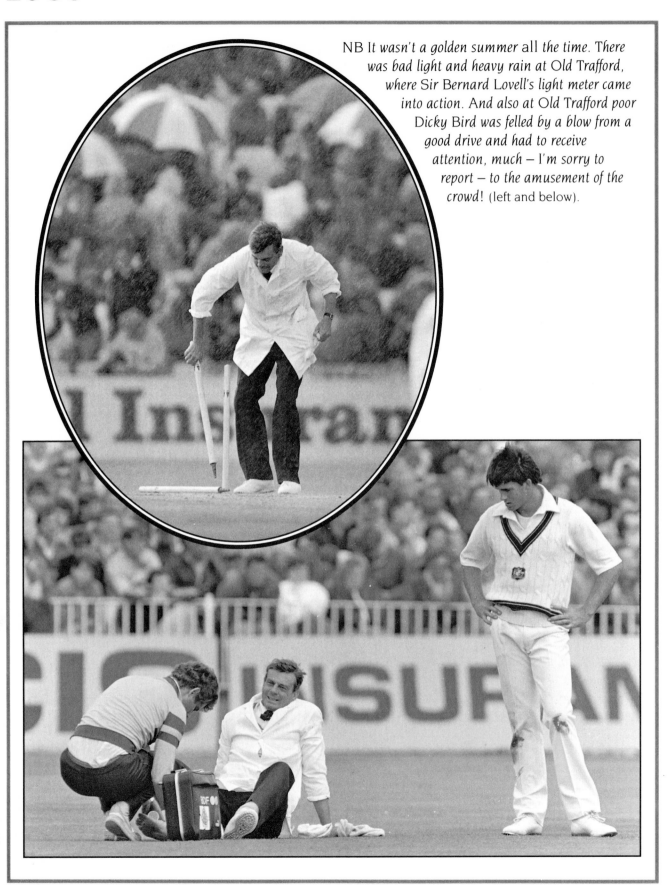

NB It wasn't a golden summer all the time. There was bad light and heavy rain at Old Trafford, where Sir Bernard Lovell's light meter came into action. And also at Old Trafford poor Dicky Bird was felled by a blow from a good drive and had to receive attention, much – I'm sorry to report – to the amusement of the crowd! (left and below).

The euphoria over the 1985 summer was too good to last. It was immediately followed by another 'blackwash' by the West Indies over David Gower's team, during the winter in the West Indies. Then came this depressing season for English cricket. Nothing seemed to go right. England lost 0–2 to India and 0–1 to New Zealand.

India won the first Test at Lord's by 5 wickets, and David Gower was docked of the captaincy. As so often seems to happen, David heard that Mike Gatting was going to succeed him, before he himself had been told that he had lost the job! Both in this Test and in the second at Headingley we saw two fine hundreds by Dilip Vengsarkar (below), his 126 not out at Lord's being his third in a Test Match at Lord's. He is a tall upright batsman with all the strokes, and there was a ring of class about all he did. He averaged 90.00 for the series and was well supported by the other batsmen, though strangely Sunny Gavaskar had a moderate tour for such a great player, averaging only 29.16.

The Indian bowling was steady with four bowlers picking up over 10 wickets each. Kapil Dev was another who had rather a disappointing tour but it was a joy to see Maninder Singh, the 21-year-old left-arm spinner, in his Bedi-like patka, being so successful, especially at Lord's where in England's second innings he had remarkable figures for an inexperienced spinner: 20.4–12–9–3

India was a happy team and popular tourists. I managed to have some fun with two nicknames which I'm glad to say they enjoyed. In fact on one day I got a message from one of their players asking if he could have a nickname too! Anyway the two I liked most were:

'Snake', for Chetan Sharma
'One Arm', for C.S. Pandit

I hope you get them!

What about England? Alas, they lost in three and a half days at Headingley under their new captain Mike Gatting (below), but did better at The Oval where Gatting's 183 not out enabled them to make exactly the same first innings total as India — 390. Had rain not interfered, either side might have won.

They did slightly better against New Zealand. A commanding 183 by Graham Gooch at Lord's and centuries by Gower and Gatting at The Oval enabled them to draw these two Tests, but they were comprehensively beaten at Trent Bridge. Richard Hadlee (right) took 19 wickets in the series with 6 in the first innings at Lord's,

and another 6 in the first innings at Trent Bridge. He bowled off his shorter run and with his accuracy, late swing, plus the ability to move the ball off the seam either way, he often seemed to mesmerise the England batsmen. Quite simply the answer is that he is a great bowler.

It was good to see Martin Crowe (left) confirm his world class as a batsman at Lord's with 106, and off-spinner John Bracewell making his first Test hundred at Trent Bridge (110). Just as useful for New Zealand but not so much fun to watch was a seven hour 119 by John Wright at The Oval.

One or two unusual happenings occurred during the season.

In the India Test at Headingley there was, due to injuries, a constant toing and froing of the India players on to the field. So it wasn't perhaps surprising that for one whole over they actually had twelve men on the field — something I had never seen in a Test Match.

There was also some confusion over the interpretation of the laws in New Zealand's second Test at Trent Bridge. When New Zealand required 1 run to win, David Gower was put on by Mike Gatting to bowl the next over. With his first delivery he deliberately 'chucked' the ball and was immediately no-balled by the square-leg umpire. This meant of course that New Zealand had won. But Martin Crowe, who was 44 not out, complicated matters by hitting the ball for 4. So the question was, since New Zealand had already won, did it count? There was general uncertainty at the time even among the umpires, but it was finally decided by TCCB that it should count. A correct decision? Surely, since the ball does not become 'dead' when a no-ball is called.

It would have been different had the umpire at the bowler's end immediately called 'time', but as it was, Martin Crowe was duly credited with 48 not out in the record books.

There had been an even more bizarre occurrence at Lord's which was a good example of the sporting and friendly relationship between England and New Zealand.

1986

Bruce French, England's wicket-keeper, had been hit hard on his helmet by a bouncer from Richard Hadlee and felt very groggy. So at the start of New Zealand's innings Bill Athey deputised as wicket-keeper. Bob Taylor, (right and below) England's old wicket-keeper, happened to be in the ground in his capacity as P.R.O. for Cornhill. He was, in fact, tucking into a late lunch when he was summoned to the English dressing-room. Coney had sportingly agreed that he should be allowed to take over behind the stumps: a generous interpretation of the laws.

Even more extraordinary, Bobby Parks of Hampshire was called to Lord's, and in turn took over from Bob Taylor. Bob, at the age of 45, had kept wicket beautifully for over seventy overs, wearing other people's trousers, shirt, box, boots and socks. But like a true wicket-keeper he always carried his own gloves around with him — just in case!

As a matter of interest, an experimental law on substitutes now lays down that no substitute shall act as wicket-keeper, probably as a result of this extraordinary incident.

Finally, it wasn't all bad news for England. In the last Test at The Oval against New Zealand, Ian Botham was recalled to the England side, and immediately showed that he had lost none of his skill and crowd appeal.

1. He took a wicket with his first ball.

2. In his second over he took another and so passed Dennis Lillee's total of 355 Test wickets (above).

3. He made a typical 59 not out (off 36 balls) with his usual ferocious drives and hooks. He took 17 off Hadlee's first two overs with the new ball, and also hit Derek Stirling for 24 runs off one over hitting 4,6,4,6,.,4. He equalled with Andy Roberts and Sandeep Patil the record for most runs off a six-ball over in a Test. It was a splendid come-back by one of Test cricket's greatest all-rounders.

1987

The rains came and virtually washed out the first two Tests against Pakistan. They won the third at Headingley easily by an innings, and with the last two drawn they won their first ever series in England.

It wasn't just the rain which made it an unhappy season until it was mercifully rescued by the MCC Bicentenary Match at Lord's. There was none of the friendliness that had existed in the previous summer. There was too much needle and unnecessary comments about the umpiring. The nationalistic fervour to win by some countries was making Test cricket into a battlefield.

This was a pity because Pakistan had some fine cricketers, none more so than their captain, the charismatic Imran Khan (below, left). Despite early injuries he took 21 wickets in the four Tests in which he bowled. Like Richard Hadlee, he is no longer so fast, but with his experience and control is probably a better bowler. Certainly, he was largely responsible for the Pakistan victory at Headingley where he took 10 wickets in the match during which he also passed a total of 300 Test wickets.

The next most effective Pakistan bowler was the 21-year-old fast left-arm Wasim Akram (below, right). With

his whippy action he picked up 16 wickets, and also showed signs of being a powerful hitter. Personally, I was disappointed that my favourite leg-spinner Abdul Qadir (left) did not do better. He did take 11 wickets but was very expensive at over 40 runs per wicket.

The Pakistan batting was consistently good, Javed Miandad (below) being outstanding with an average of 72.00. He is really a remarkably fine player but his temperament does not endear him to his opponents in any country.

Mike Gatting was the best batsman for England, finishing strongly with a century in each of the last two Tests.

In his 150 not out at The Oval he saved England from what might have been an horrendous innings defeat, after Pakistan had made 708. His partner was a strangely quiet Ian Botham, who having had an unsuccessful series, played here with responsibility and good sense making 51 not out in over four hours.

Neil Foster and Graham Dilley took 15 and 14 wickets respectively and were by far the best of the English bowlers. Neil was especially good at Headingley where he took advantage of the conditions and swung the ball on a full length. He bowled his heart out and thoroughly deserved his best ever Test figures of 46.2–15–107–8.

So much for the series against Pakistan, but as I said the chef-d'oeuvres was to come. It was Bicentenary year for MCC and there were numerous celebratory lunches, dinners and, in March, a Bicentenary Ball at Lord's. It was to have been held in a vast marquee on the nursery end but the night before there was a tremendous storm and the marquee was blown down. By a speedy and efficient military operation everything was transferred to the pavilion, and we found ourselves dancing to Joe Loss and his band in the Real Tennis Court! It was a wonderful evening, miraculously saved by the MCC staff.

The Bicentenary Match of MCC v. the Rest of the World was even better and we enjoyed three full days of glorious sunshine. Alas we paid for it on the fifth day when it pelted down and there was no play possible at all. A great pity, because the Rest of the World had been set 353 to win and had lost 1 wicket for 13 at the close of the fourth day. But disappointing as it was the memory of the rest of the match made up for it, and anyway the result never really mattered. It was the cricket which lived up to the occasion and with all the great modern Test cricketers playing (except Viv Richards who was contracted to play for Rishton in the Lancashire league), it was one of the most enjoyable games of cricket which I have ever seen. All the top skills were there and everyone was trying their hardest. But it was all played in the most friendly and sporting way. Looking back I can think of no dissent on umpires' decisions, no time-wasting, no animosity on the field and only the occasional legitimate bouncer. It was just the way cricket at Test match level should be played but sadly seldom is.

For me the highlights of this memorable game were:

1. The batting of Gooch, Gatting and Greenidge (opposite, top) for MCC, all making centuries.

2. The sight of Marshall (opposite, below) bowling at his most venomous to Gavaskar, batting in what he said was to be the end of his Test match career. He was the supreme master even among all the other great players present. He made 188 in six and three quarter hours and hit 22 fours. Everyone had hoped that he would get the double century which would have been a fitting climax to his career. But it was not to be. He gave a return catch to a flighted ball from Ravish Shastri. I am sure that Ravish was as sorry as anyone, as Sunny had been his hero for the last fifteen years or so. Imran Khan gave Sunny great support in a partnership of 180, in over a run a minute, of which Imran made 82.

And finally there was one of the best pieces of fielding I have been lucky enough to see. Gooch was 117, and the bowler was the tall West Indian off spinner Roger Harper. Gooch went down the wicket and drove him firmly back. Harper fielded the ball and in one movement flung down Gooch's wicket. Gooch stood there helpless and in amazement. It was a lightning piece of fielding and Gooch was the first to congratulate Harper.

I have so many happy memories of the match I only wish I could be there commentating on the Tercentenary

match in 2087. But I rather doubt if I shall be around.

Postscript. Nineteen eighty-seven was a very personal year for me. On the day after the Lord's Test I celebrated my seventy-fifth birthday. Optimistically, a day early, the MCC presented me with a super cake decorated with a cricket match (below). What made it so special was that it was personally delivered to me by the MCC.

HAPPY BIRTHDAY JOHNNERS 75 NOT OUT!

1987

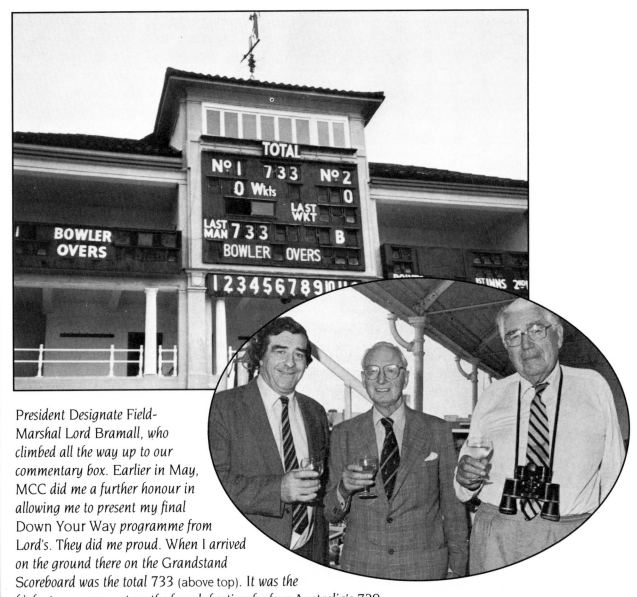

President Designate Field-Marshal Lord Bramall, who climbed all the way up to our commentary box. Earlier in May, MCC did me a further honour in allowing me to present my final Down Your Way programme from Lord's. They did me proud. When I arrived on the ground there on the Grandstand Scoreboard was the total 733 (above top). It was the highest score ever put on the board, beating by four Australia's 729 in 1930. I interviewed six people to represent MCC: Colin Cowdrey, then the President; the Secretary John Stephenson; the Curator Stephen Green; the head groundsman Mick Hunt; Nancy Doyle, who produces the best 'table' on the first-class circuit; and last of all one of Lord's greatest sons, Denis Compton. It was a marvellous farewell to a programme which I had presented for 15 years.

Just one more mention of the Bicentenary Match. We were lucky that many of the great cricketers playing came up to visit us in the commentary box - even Sunny Gavaskar after his long innings. A nostalgic moment and one I know thoroughly appreciated by our listeners was a commentary à deux by Rex Alston and Jim Swanton (seen above with Fred Trueman). They were as good as ever even after such a long absence: Rex said he had done his last Test commentary 23 years ago. He even got a wicket when he described Shastri's caught and bowled off Gavaskar. To complete the nostalgia, we spoke on the telephone to John Arlott in Alderney. What happy memories of T.M.S. it all brought back!

I have enjoyed commentating so much that it is only when I look back as I am doing now that I realise what a disastrous time the last half of the 1980s has been for England. They have been beaten at home by all the Test playing countries except Sri Lanka, who didn't do too badly in their first Test here in 1984.

Nineteen eighty-eight was a typical year, West Indies winning four of the five Tests. Once again their fast bowling was too much for our batsmen. Malcolm Marshall had a highly successful tour taking 35 wickets supported by a 6 feet 7 inch newcomer, Curtly Ambrose (overleaf), who took 22. Only Gooch and Lamb could look back with any satisfaction: both averaging over 40 and scoring one century each.

In contrast, five West Indies batsmen averaged 47 or over, with little Gus Logie topping them all with 72·80. Viv Richards had a disappointing tour and strangely only one hundred was made – by Greenidge. But the batting was consistent and due to England's small totals West Indies were not called on to make big totals. England made under 206 seven times, which gives some idea of the West Indies' superiority. In fact, had Marshall not had a rib injury during England's second innings at Trent Bridge, West Indies might have made a clean sweep.

Marshall has Gooch caught by Dujon at Headingley

1988

But to be fair to England they did have a lot of injuries, so prevalent these days in spite of the half hour or so of physical jerks they do on each morning of a Test. The selectors had to call on 23 players and, even worse, on four different captains. This was less excusable. Even after his unfortunate fracas with the Pakistan umpire Shakoor Rana during the winter, Mike Gatting (above, left) started as Captain. But he was unwise or naive enough to take a barmaid up to his room during the Trent Bridge Test. Not very clever, with the press staying in the same hotel. The selectors said that they believed his story that nothing untoward had happened, and then promptly sacked him! John Emburey (above, centre) took over for the next two Tests and was then replaced at Headingley by Chris Cowdrey, (above, right) selected for his leadership qualities and with an eye on the future. Unfortunately it made no difference. England lost by 10 wickets, and Chris himself only made 0 and 5. He was then injured during Canterbury Week and Graham Gooch (right) became England's fourth captain for the Oval Test. Although he made an uncharacteristic 84 in just over seven hours, trying to bolster up England's second innings, they still lost by 8 wickets.

There was some slight cheer for England supporters when Sri Lanka were beaten at Lord's in their only Test. But at least they kept play going until just after lunch on the last day. This produced an amusing situation. Essex were starting a four day match against Surrey at The Oval, and Keith Fletcher decided to put Surrey in, and fielded with only ten men. What faith in Gooch's value to Essex! So Gooch became the first man to captain his country in a Test until after lunch, and then to play for his county for the rest of the same day.

161

1989

How wrong can one be! Before the series against Australia started I – and a lot of other people too – forecast that it would be a hard fought series between two not very good but even sides. It was also agreed that except for Sri Lanka, they were both joint bottom of the league of Test playing countries.

So why were we so wrong? Why did Australia outplay England so completely and win 4–0 and with easily the best of the two draws?

Above: Merv Hughes triumphant

1. Australia owed a great deal to their cricket manager, Bobby Simpson. He insisted on the players employing the basic techniques such as playing with straight bats and, even more important, with lighter bats, with a maximum weight of 2lbs 7oz. He put a premium on supreme physical fitness – and as a result they were able to play the same team in five of the six Tests, only calling on twelve players. Another vital factor was the way that he and Allan Border instilled the will to win so that the tour became something of a crusade. There can have been few visiting sides with a better team spirit.

2. Border himself led the side superbly and both his tactics and the handling of his bowlers were difficult to fault.

3. The batting was a mixture of brilliance and solidity and never failed. Incredibly, they made over 600 twice, over 500 once and three times over 400. It may have been a coincidence, but unlike the England batsmen, all the Australians stood at the crease with their bats on the ground, not held aloft like a baseball player. The oustanding performers were Steve Waugh (right) with an average of 126.50, two hundreds and a model technique which all schoolboys could follow. His 177 not out at Headingley was his first hundred in 27 Tests. He followed it at Lord's with 152 not out and 21 not out. So it wasn't until he was bowled by Fraser at Edgbaston in the third Test for 43 that he had a batting average – a mere 393!

More flamboyant and a joy to watch was Dean Jones (right),who also made two hundreds and averaged over 70. A feature of the series was the brilliant running between the wickets by Waugh and Jones especially. It was another basic – always run the first run fast. Border and Boon both would have topped the averages on a normal tour and were consistent and seldom failed. But the outstanding success of them all was Mark Taylor (above), a sound solid left-hander with a superb temperament and perfect technique. He enjoyed occupying the crease as much as Boycott used to. His 839 runs included a vitally important hundred in the first Test at Headingley, and a magnificent 219 at Trent Bridge where he and Geoff Marsh put on 329 for the 1st wicket.

4. Border only had to rely on four bowlers, two fast, one swing and a leg spinner. The quickies were Geoff Lawson (above) with 29 wickets, and Merv Hughes (left) with 19; and Trevor Holmes with his leg spinners accounted for 11. But the star of the series was undoubtedly Terry Alderman (opposite page) who, with his accurate outswingers and his devastating 'nipper back' took 41 wickets — one fewer than he had taken in 1981! He completely bemused the England batsmen and had the remarkable total of 19 lbws given in his favour. When I was in Australia the following winter they were saying there that they thought that our umpires had been over-generous to him on occasions. But nothing can take away his deadly accurate line and length, coupled with his late swing.

1989

There is little that I can honestly say in praise of England. David Gower (above) was appointed captain for all six Tests, but as disaster followed disaster he did not have the aggressive leadership so badly needed to rally his troops. He laughs about it, but however much he cared and worried underneath, outwardly he was too laid back. His first and vital mistake was to put Australia in at Headingley in the first Test. They made 601 for 7 dec. and after that England were never in the hunt. I am sure that their team spirit and will to win were affected by the intrigues which were secretly going on about the tour to South Africa. Once again, there was a flood of injuries and 29 players were used in the series – six more than in 1988.

Neil Foster had the doubtful honour of being the most successful bowler with just 12 wickets at 35.08 each. No one else got into double figures!

Robin Smith (opposite, above), with 553 runs at 61.44, had a very good series and several times lifted our hearts, especially with his 96 at Lord's, 143 at Old Trafford and 101 at Trent Bridge. David Gower was typically inconsistent but played one lovely innings of 106 at Lord's. The surprise success was wicket-keeper Jack Russell (opposite, below). He had made 94 in his first Test at Lord's against Sri Lanka in 1988 and surpassed this with his first Test hundred (128 not out) at Old Trafford. He is a left-hander, has a basically sound defence and plays sensibly within his limitations. His wicket-keeping was one of the bright spots in a fielding side which did not compare with Australia in speed and throwing.

It is sad to have to write so many critical things about England. They did, though, have one genuine excuse. Allan Lamb, after making a hard hit 125 with 24 fours at Headingley, could not play in any of the other Tests due to injury. Oh, and I suppose England could justifiably say that the gloriously hot and fine summer was of more benefit to the Australians.

But what it really all came down to was that the faulty technique of the England batsmen was glaringly exposed, and was further proof of how much harm one-day cricket has done to batsmen in this country. They don't play straight, they try to steer the ball through the slips area and because of the heavy bats which they use, they have to hold them in the air at the ready. I must admit that for once I felt very depressed by the end of the season. At least 1990 could not be any worse.

1990

New Zealand

This summer made up for the disappointments of the last few seasons. England had regained some confidence after their performance in the West Indies, and our two visitors were New Zealand and India – two countries who play entertaining cricket in a friendly way.

After all the aggression, and barrage of bouncers in the West Indies, cricket lovers were hoping for something more like their idea of how cricket should be played.

Except for the weather during the New Zealand series, their hopes were fulfilled, and by the end of August we were able to look back on a hot summer of entertaining cricket, matched by the sporting spirit in which it was played.

During the first Test at Trent Bridge there were constant interruptions for rain and bad light and the match was drawn – New Zealand 208 and 36 for 2, England 345 for 9 dec. For England Mike Atherton (below) made an impressive 151, and Philip DeFreitas took 5 for 53 – his best Test figures – bowling outswingers on a moist Saturday morning. For New Zealand the new cricketing knight Sir Richard Hadlee, in spite of a hand injury took four wickets, including Grahan Gooch lbw off the first ball of the England innings. Hadlee was the twelfth cricketer to be knighted, and the first to be honoured whilst still playing Test cricket (opposite, top left, seen receiving congratulations for his 431st Test wicket in the third Test).

In the second Test at Lord's the weather once again prevented a definite result, though the large crowd saw England, who were put into bat, play some delightfully attractive cricket to make 334. This time it was Mike Atherton who made 0, with Graham Gooch starting his prolific sequence of Test scores with a commanding innings of 85.

New Zealand replied with 462 for 9 dec. thanks largely to an opening partnership of 185 between Trevor Franklin (101) and John Wright (98). Even the England team would have liked John (above, right) to get his hundred on his last Test appearance at Lord's. He is one of the nicest and most popular of cricketers.

Sir Richard pitched in with a typically aggressive 86, including a huge straight six over the sightscreen. It was off Gladstone Small just after he had started with the second new ball.

Devon Malcolm (left) bowled fast with plenty of bounce and took 5 for 94, so New Zealand did well to lead by 128 runs.

When England batted again Allan Lamb played an exuberant innings of 84 supported by a steady 54 by Mike Atherton to make up for his 0 in the first innings.

England won the third and last Test at Edgbaston by 114 runs and so won the first home series in this country since 1985. England was, strangely, put in by John Wright and made 435 with Graham Gooch (154) and Mike Atherton (82) putting on 170 for the first wicket. New Zealand were all out for 249 thanks to some fine off-spin bowling by Eddie Hemmings (right) on a pitch which took spin. He finished with 6 for 58, his best ever Test figures.

England, going for quick runs made only 158 in the second innings, thanks to a magnificent farewell performance by Sir Richard, who took 5 for 53. This gave him a Test total of 431 wickets with an average of 5 wickets in each of his 86 Tests. What a great bowler he has been. A short run up, perfect sideways-on action, deadly accurate line and length, and the ability to swing the ball away from the batsman, and then suddenly to swing one in unexpectedly. A fine sportsman and a worthy knight.

Set 345 to win, New Zealand had to face a fast and fiery Devon Malcolm who took 5 for 46 to give him 15 wickets in the series.

What a pity the weather prevented more than one definite result. Even with Mark Greatbatch and Martin Crowe strangely out of form, the teams were still very evenly matched.

Champagne Moments

Nineteen eighty-nine was the centenary of the Savoy Hotel. As part of their celebrations they asked me and the Test Match Special team to choose a Champagne Moment in each Test, and the best hundred in the series. The prize for the winner – i.e. the player concerned in the Champagne Moment – was a jeroboam of Pol Roger Champagne. The best century-maker got a dozen bottles.

In 1990 Veuve Cliquot took over, and the prize became a jeroboam of Veuve Cliquot.

A Champagne Moment could be a brilliant catch or run-out, a gigantic hit for six, an unplayable ball, or an important milestone reached by a particular player.

The winners in 1989 were Merv Hughes, Robin Smith, Angus Fraser, Jack Russell, Mark Taylor and David Gower. In 1990 the winners were Michael Atherton, Richard Hadlee (below left) , Graham Gooch, Kapil Dev (bottom), Sachim Tendulkar (below, right) and David Gower again. Here are photos of some of the winners.

1990

India

The second series was an Indian Summer, which I shall never forget. Gorgeous weather, fantastic stroke play, spinners bowling again in Test cricket and three sporting encounters to provide the sun-drenched crowds with great entertainment.

In the first Test at Lord's the Indian Captain Azharuddin won the toss and like John Wright at Edgbaston, put England in to bat. With the same result! England won easily by 247 runs. They made 653 for 4 dec., Gooch (333) playing a wonderful innings of power and concentration (below). *He was well supported by Allan Lamb (139) and Robin Smith (100*) but it will always be known as Gooch's match. In England's second innings he made 123 giving him a total of 456 for the match - a new record for any Test. He also became the first batsman to score a triple century and a century in the same match. His 333 was the highest score ever made at Lord's and the highest by a Test captain.*

India's reaction to England's large total was remarkable. Instead of a long defensive grind, I saw one of the best Test hundreds in all my 45 summers – 121 by Azharuddin (above, left). It was full of grace, exquisite timing and wristy strokes. He played the ball late, and often turned it from outside the off-stump to mid-wicket, with a last minute twist of the wrists. His hundred came off only 87 balls. Shastri going in first was the necessary sheet anchor with exactly 100. Kapil Dev (above, right) then came in at No. 8 to thrill the large crowd with a remarkable display of hitting. With nine wickets down and Hirwani at the other end, India needed exactly 24 runs to save the follow-on. Kapil Dev proceeded to drive Eddie Hemmings for four successive straight sixes – the last one clearing the sightscreen and landing far beyond. The next ball, Hirwani was out for 0 and Kapil Dev had saved the follow-on by one run. His 77 not out was worthy of Jessop or Botham at their best.

In England's seconnd innings, in addition to Gooch's 123, Mike Atherton made 72, and together they put on 204 for the first wicket to enable England to declare at 272 for 4. Allan Lamb was caught by one of the most spectacular catches I have ever seen. The 17-year-old Tendulkar ran at least 30 yards from long off, catching the ball with his right hand stretched out in front of him.

India could not repeat their first innings brilliance however, and were all out for 224, England winning by 247 runs.

The match was also a personal triumph for Angus Fraser (above left) who with his accurate line and length took eight wickets in the two innings on his home ground. If only he had been selected for the Lord's Test in 1989!

The second Test at Old Trafford saw another high scoring match with England making 519, Gooch 116, Atherton 131 and Smith 121* all making hundreds with another double century partnership of 225 between Gooch and Atherton.

India replied with their usual panache thanks to a fine 93 by Manjhekar, a promising 68 by Tendulkar (above, right) and best of all another superb innings (179) of wristy stoke play by Azharuddin. They finished 87 runs behind and with England declaring 320 for 4 India were set 408 to win. This time it had been Allan Lamb's turn for a hundred in which he showed that his first innings nightmare against the two leg-spinners was too bad to be true. And incidentally what a joy it was to see Hirwani and Kumble – two leg-spinners – bowling in tandem, and they were rewarded with eight wickets between them in the match.

At 183 for 6 it looked as if India would lose. But a fine partnership between Tendulkar (119*) and Prabhakar (67) enabled them to draw at 343 for 6. This was young Tendulkar's maiden Test hundred and he became the second youngest player to achieve one, Mushtaq Mohammad being the youngest. He batted like a veteran with remarkable judgement and temperament, and with a classical technique. He will surely be the

Gavaskar of the future. Indeed Sunny has said that Tendulkar is better than he was at that age. Tendulkar first played first-class cricket when aged 14. He does not drink, nor smoke, is not yet interested in girls (though they are interested in him!) and he goes to bed at 10.30. That sounds like dedication to me!

And so to The Oval for the third Test, which India had to win to square the series. This time in winning the toss Azharuddin decided to bat. To show what might have happened at Lord's had he done so there, India stroked their way to 606 for 9 dec. Shastri was once again the anchor man scoring 187 in seven hours. The stroke play came from Kapil Dev (110) and Azharuddin (78).

In spite of another captain's innings by Graham Gooch (85), the other early England batsmen failed and it needed Robin Smith (57) and Eddie Hemmings (51) to take England's score to 340 – 266 runs behind. I must not forget Devon Malcolm's 15 not out, which included a giant six over long-on, off Hirwani (above). The crowd loved it. So did Devon!

When England followed on it was back to normal, with Gooch scoring 88 and Atherton 86, sharing another big opening partnership of 176. After Gooch was out on Monday evening David Gower (right) came in with his whole future depending on how he did. He made a graceful and beautifully timed 32 that evening and then on the last day went on to make his sixteenth Test hundred. When stumps were drawn he had made 157 not out, and with 7674 runs passed Colin Cowdrey's total and became the second highest scorer for England, after Geoff Boycott (8114).

1990

All day on Tuesday he showed great restraint and judgement and undoubtedly played himself into the England team going to Australia. The excellent last day crowd gave him a tremendous standing ovation lasting at least two minutes when he reached his hundred. They – and he – were relieved and delighted after all the speculation about his future. One felt that the prodigal son had returned.

England finished at 477 for 4 dec. An amazing feature of their second innings was that India's acting captain, Shastri, kept leg-spinner Hirwani on for 59 overs unchanged from the Vauxhall end, and never took the second new ball. The one ball used notched up 154 overs!

And so the match was drawn and England had won the series 1–0. What a perfect Indian Summer it had been, and what a happy way to finish 45 summers in the commentary box.